DOGMATIC

DOGMATIC

Featuring Dusty Rhodes, the K9 Kid, and
the Doberman Who Didn't Like Doughnuts

GERRY BURKE

DOGMATIC
FEATURING DUSTY RHODES, THE K9 KID, AND THE
DOBERMAN WHO DIDN'T LIKE DOUGHNUTS

iUniverse books may be ordered through booksellers or by contacting:

iUniverse
1663 Liberty Drive
Bloomington, IN 47403
www.iuniverse.com
844-349-9409

ISBN: 978-1-6632-5573-0 (sc)
ISBN: 978-1-6632-5574-7 (hc)
ISBN: 978-1-6632-5575-4 (e)

Library of Congress Control Number: 2023916133

Print information available on the last page.

iUniverse rev. date: 09/18/2023

CONTENTS

CONTENTS

A SMALL TOWN

Dave Rhodes was the kind of husband who gave his wife a vacuum cleaner for her birthday. The kids didn't do surprises and knew what they wanted. Gifts could be found scattered all over the house, including game devices, Barbie dolls, and enough anti-alien laser guns to repel Darth Vadar and a million Stormtroopers. After a pre-Christmas think-tank meeting, the three children decided they deserved a dog. Realising their father might want to resist the opportunity to expand the family in this way, the boys charged Chloe, five, with the job of bringing him around to their way of thinking. Another mouth to feed might stretch the budget, but the youngsters would be prepared to give up their portions of spinach and other green edibles if it would help.

It has to be said that Chloe was the Mata Hari of five-year-olds. Using all her feminine charms, she possessed the ability to turn her father into a compliant servant within minutes of locking her arms around his neck. With the commitment confirmed, the eldest son, Rory, stepped in to declare that he had prize-picked a potential candidate for the yet-to-be-purchased kennel. The father of his best mate at school, a grazier, owned a spread the envy of most folks in the area. The litter of pups would be there for the taking, and it would cost Dave nothing. Nevertheless, he did question the need for this breed.

"A sheepdog! I know we live on a farm, but we only have one sheep. Are you sure?"

Shawn may have been a single entity but he was no ordinary sheep. He possessed half a brain and a dynamic personality, and interacted well with the children. Mrs Rhodes, less keen, considered buying her husband a lawn mower for Christmas. In this way, they might get to enjoy roast lamb instead of the usual boring ham.

The family lived on a rural property, but don't paint Dave as a farmer. The fellow sold farm machinery. His wife, Annie, supplemented their income with her various cottage industries, which included door sales of eggs (chicken and duck), fruit, and feather-down quilts.

Did she think the backyard would become more chaotic with ducks, chooks, a sheep, and now a dog? Yes, she did, but young Chloe could be persuasive.

The puppy arrived in a basket with a bow tied around his neck, with the sound of departing sleigh bells in the distance. Rory took charge and introduced the little fella to every member of the family. The young girl provided similar introductions to each of her dolls. Dusty licked them all and then retreated to the fireplace, where he discovered a large bone wrapped in Christmas tinsel. The children believed it would be best to initiate the tyke into the joys of the yuletide season, so he might enjoy it as much as they did.

Over the ensuing months, the pup kept close to his three protectors as he felt vulnerable outside, at the mercy of loud and inconsiderate farm animals. Protecting one's patch is quite the thing with creatures, often wary of any new arrival. Of course, adventures could be encountered beyond the perimeter of the property, but all in good time.

The puppy didn't have a lot to do with Mr and Mrs Rhodes, although he must have wondered why the woman continually followed him with a green plastic bag. This would all change when he became older and wiser. Two years down the track and Annie wouldn't go to town without her faithful companion by her side. On these occasions, the dog would get to meet the townspeople, and they all loved him.

On her shopping excursions, the country housewife couldn't take the pet into the supermarket, so she tied him up on the footpath. The shopkeeper next door didn't like this much because he thought the dishlicker deterred customers, so he always untied the barking beast. The liberated animal then proceeded to freewheel down High Street on a voyage of discovery, which included the butcher shop, the bakery, and Fat Al's burger joint.

In this way, new friends would be made, some of them possessing a welcoming nature and a generosity of spirit. Often, a slice of salami would come sailing out of the window of Mother Petrocelli's Deli just as Dusty passed by. It is a credit to the woofer that he always arrived back at the supermarket in time to greet his mistress with her shopping. She never noticed (or cared) that her escort was no longer tied up.

As time went by, Annie didn't bother with the pretence of tying him up, and he roamed free every Tuesday for one hour. During that time, the inquisitive dog performed many civic services, some above and beyond community expectations. For example, he always patrolled the school toilets, looking for those misfits keen to wag class. Who can forget the day the canine caught Sammy Stuyvesant and Delia Davidoff smoking? When the principal appeared on the scene, he discovered them doing more than that. Very embarrassing!

The day he saved Bernadette Brody's baby proved to be another bookmark of bravado. Mum only let go of the pram for an instant, but it started to roll down Harlequin Hill, picking up speed with every wheel rotation. The two Rhodes scholars, Rory and Jake, saw what was happening from the schoolyard but expected Superman to intervene. Yes, they also believed in the Easter bunny.

On the back of "kiss and go," man's best friend prepared to join Annie in the family vehicle when he observed the pram careering down the road and went after it.

You may have heard the stories, some of them embellished. Dusty couldn't run faster than a speeding bullet, but he did stretch out and caught up with the baby carriage before it smashed into the water faucet at the end of the road. The dog couldn't stop the impetus of the four-wheeler, but he jumped aboard and sunk his teeth into the swaddling clothes around the baby's neck. The fearless one broke free with the child with seconds to spare and then delivered the crying infant back to her mother. What a hero!

Annie couldn't have been prouder of the sheepdog, but the explanation to her husband didn't come out right.

"What are you talking about, sweetheart? Dusty delivered a baby?"

The Four Paws Society existed because of the number of dog owners in town and out. They represented every political persuasion, so agreement on anything proved difficult. In matters of respect, no disagreement existed as to who was their star. However, the suggestion from Kimberly Carruthers came from left field.

"Ladies, gentlemen, fellow members, I would like to recommend that we endorse Dusty Rhodes as our candidate in the forthcoming council election."

Nice one, Kimberly.

Mmmm, quite interesting. The incumbent in their ward, Bruce Pickles, was the mayor but on the nose for all kinds of reasons. Few people thought he would be able to retain his position, but could he be beaten by a dog?

Some years ago in Australia, the politician Bill Hayden declared that "a drover's dog could lead the Labor Party to victory." The Four Paw representative might admit to being more Liberal than Labor, but there's a precedent, if you need one. At the Rhodes property, the working dog only droved one sheep, so he had time on his hands.

The vulnerability of Bruce Pickles needs to be explained. Three years earlier, the out-of-favour mayor presented as a shining light, elected in a landslide. At the time, nobody knew him to be a paedophile with a criminal record for fraud and aggravated assault. To avoid such issues, one often chooses to relocate, and this is what Bruce and his wife did. Yes, all hail the forgiving wife, every bit as gullible as he might have hoped.

The accountant's job at Sullivan and Sons appealed, as did the sons, Dan and Tim, earmarked for managerial roles in about fifteen years. Sullivan's, the best (and only) furniture store in town, was expensive, but nobody questioned the quality of their merchandise. The pencil pusher should have been concealed in the back office, but he harboured this desire to strut about the premises and bond with the customers. Rather than describe the fellow, let me quote from *My Fair Lady*.

"Oozing charm from every pore, he oiled his way around the floor."

Some of these people he recognised from the Valley Church of Praise, where he held the position of honorary treasurer and lead vocalist. To them, Bruce wasn't the sleaze that many people thought, and he did have a fine tenor voice. The parishioners were more than happy to support his push at politics and would only find out about his crimes after election day.

The death of Mrs Pickles came as a shock and must be described as a sad affair, with most people believing the husband to be responsible. Of course he was responsible. You should never point a gun at anybody, even if you only intended to clean it. What was this guy doing with a gun, you ask?

It would have been nice if the police asked the same question, but they didn't. The station chief played golf with the suspect and declared him to be a rum fellow, so they exonerated him. The pastor at the Church of Praise also confirmed this characterisation when funds went missing from the weekly collection. The chap was having a dream run, but would the fickle finger of fate soon dial M for mayor? The odds were not in his favour.

You rarely meet people with delusions of grandeur in a small regional town because country folks have a way of cutting you down to size. Somehow, Bruce slipped through the cracks. I cite the general disharmony in chambers when he exchanged his chair for a throne. You can do that if you're in the furniture business.

What about the junket to Japan to investigate the possibility of starting up a Wasabi plantation where the sewerage treatment plant used to be? Lucinda Quinlan, the token Greenie on the council, should have been the one to undertake this investigative journey.

You guessed it. Mayor Pickles intervened, upgraded the only ticket to first class, and frolicked among the apple blossoms, before eating his way around the various sushi trains in Kyoto and Tokyo. With little time allocated for due diligence, the sad truth emerged. Wasabi requires a warm, humid climate to thrive. Some people would describe the sewage location as all of that, but it was not appropriate for this part of Victoria. The disappointed traveller retreated to his favourite Onsen and sat in a bath until the flying kangaroo (Qantas) arrived to return him home.

He would also be in hot water when he arrived back in chambers to discover a revolt amongst his constituents after someone leaked details of his previous history. With elections on the horizon, the mayor became a liability to himself and his prospects. The question on everybody's lips— "Who would oppose him?"

The most popular person in town was Basil Green, proprietor of the fashionable franchise "Murder by Chocolate." Situated on top of Harlequin Hill, the shop of enchantment delighted many. If you survived the climb, a reward seemed appropriate, and Basil and his wife were never short of customers. Notwithstanding his popularity, Rosemary refused to allow her husband to be involved in politicking of any kind, as politics polarised the community and could mean a loss of trade.

When the election flyers for the nominee were distributed, no one questioned the picture of a dog, front and centre, because the candidate had been endorsed by the Four Paws Society. Most people remembered Mr Rhodes but forgot his name was Dave, not Dusty. Dave's appearance at the polling booths didn't lessen the confusion in any way.

So, it came to pass that Dusty was elected, but you don't become top dog just because you defeated the former office-bearer. The reluctant politician became mayor because the other councillors couldn't agree on a suitable person for the position; the popular pooch became the compromise candidate. On entering chambers, the animal made a beeline for the throne and refused to be moved. Could anyone want a more defining endorsement?

Looking back at his first hundred days, one could be impressed by some of the initiatives passed by these servants of the shire, not the least being their campaign to clean up the streets. "Prevent Peeing in Public," a program directed at various loose bladder delinquents in the town, proved popular, and the councillors named and shamed the most blatant offenders, such as Mrs Coates' goats and Georgia Klingner's cats, who roamed around the streets as if they owned the place. Getting Dusty to pee by example would be another thing, putting Kimberly Carruthers and the Four Paws Society under pressure.

For council meetings scheduled outside of school hours, the mayor's carers would be one of the siblings. Otherwise, Annie would be the lady with the lead. Being a wise head, she could contribute when difficult decisions were required to be made. One of these challenging resolutions involved a judgement as to whether the town would celebrate 14 February in the usual manner. The owner of the flower shop thought they should, and over at Sullivan and Sons, one man looked forward to the special day: the anniversary of the St. Valentine's Day Massacre.

Bruce, the wife-killer, only possessed one gun, which he cleaned regularly. Would he like to line up all the councillors against the wall and shoot them? Not that he should hold them responsible for his recent defeat. Insanity is a disease that precludes rational thought, so anyone would be fair game in his quest for retribution. There would be one primary target about to experience the full force of his vengeance, but Dusty was fast asleep on his throne, unaware of his predecessor's desire for satisfaction. It would be no consolation for the madman to learn that most people thought the current councillors were doing well.

"Give a dog a bone," another council initiative, found favour with the community, and they responded. So much so that one of the staff declared:

"There aren't this many bones in the graveyard."

This is when the health people stepped forward and decided that all bone donations that came to the Town Hall should be checked for salmonella. The one sent over from Sullivan and Sons should have been checked for nitro-glycerine. The bloody thing exploded when tossed into the corner pile behind the statue of Sir Henry Parkes, the Father of Federation in Australia.

The Town Hall lost the statue, plus two windows, one wall, and three mock Grecian columns, all covered by insurance. With no one killed, you might say they dodged a bullet, but nerves were on edge. At a hastily-called meeting, a resolution was passed to hire two sniffer dogs from H.M. Customs. The mayor somehow indicated that he would prefer the recruits to be female.

The investigation at the furniture store came to nothing, although information came to light that their accountant started his working career as a chemical engineer, but he never worked in an abattoir or a cemetery. How would he know about bones?

Cringing in his back office, the creepy accountant stewed in his reflections of regret. *How could he have stuffed up such a foolproof plan? What a waste of St. Valentine's Day. Bring on the Ides of March.*

You have to wonder about someone who can compare Julius Caesar standing tall in the Senate and Dusty the dog standing small in the Town Hall. The difference was that everyone was out to get Caesar; one man sought to murder the mayor. That man might prove to be just as brutal as Brutus.

In Roman times, the Ides of March didn't have a daylight-saving component attached to it, so Mr Pickles waited for the moon to go down. He realised that any self-respecting, knife-wielding assassin, should sneak up on the target in the dead of night and be wearing Hush-Puppies. Approaching the Rhodes farm on foot, he sensed the chickens were restless. Shawn the sheep pranced about nervously, and the ducks headed for the pond. Then there was the recent addition to the menagerie, Patricia, the python, a young, inexperienced, but fun-loving reptile who liked to hang out on the porch posts. The intruder would be rapt to meet her. Or not!

In his kennel on the front verandah, the designated security operative opened one eye and twitched his nose. The sensitivity of a dog's nose is thousands of times more powerful than a human's, and Bruce's body odour gave him away. Not that there seemed to be any urgency about the pooch's call to action. Slowly, he found his four feet and rose to his most formidable height. The commotion came from around the corner of the return verandah, so he padded his way to the spot where he discovered the former lord mayor grappling with Patricia, the python.

To be quite frank, Dusty and Patricia didn't get on. Before her arrival, he had been the go-to guy for food disposal and the play-time preference for Chloe and the kids. Admittedly, committee meetings kept him away from home more often, but one knows when a luminary loses his lustre. Is this the reason the dog went for the snake instead of the prowler?

Patricia had never felt pain before, and those dog bites hurt. The reptile forgot about her game with the stranger and focused her attention on the canine. She considered him the grumpiest member of the family, but he rarely resorted to violence. Perhaps if she gave him a hug, all would be well. In the end, the humans ended the fight, and the trespasser scarpered.

With all the house lights on, the family members turned up in their pyjamas and surveyed the scene. Rory discovered the shiv in the bushes, and Patricia received all the accolades (and some soothing balm for her wounds). The yard guard just retreated to his kennel, feeling unloved and unappreciated.

I know what you're thinking. Bruce, back in the safety of his abode, would be planning something further for 9/11 or 7 December (Pearl Harbour). This is how his mind worked.

This is not how my mind works. The intervention of the surly sheepdog could be a precursor to reconciliation involving the two lord mayors. After all, Dusty saved the guy from the playful python, a serpent who didn't know the difference between a cuddle and crushed vertebrae. The two political animals would meet again at the Harlequin Hill Hoedown, sponsored by the Valley Church of Praise.

The church was situated in the valley, at the bottom of the steep incline, just beyond the faucet with the pram wrapped around it. Halfway up the rise, the organisers erected a stage for the performers, with interest at an all-time high. The out-of-towners always book early because accommodation is limited. This year, several celebrated gospel singers entered the music competition, and Dolly Parton sent a message of support. In the "Thank God it's Sunday" category, the terrific tenor would lead the church choir with their rendition of "Nativity in Nashville." Dusty would be one of the judges, along with Keith Suburban and Emmylou Paris.

You can probably see the case for replacing retribution with bribery or intimidation, Pickles being capable of both. On top of that, the pastor of this church had Italian friends. Naturally, any financial corruption would have to be financed from the poor box, but the treasurer had access to the key.

The good news for Bruce was that the late Leonard Cohen would not be back with "Hallelujah," and no Elvis representative would sing "Amazing Graceland." While the choir practised for their tilt at the title, the kids in town readied themselves for their character-defining event— the billy cart charge down Harlequin Hill, sponsored by Basil Green's chocolate shop. The first prize was a mouth-watering assortment of sweets that any red-blooded adolescent would die for, and might. If comparisons could be made, I would nominate the chariot race in *Ben Hur*.

At the Rhodes farm, Rory and Jake tried to insert spikes into the wheels of their vehicle, but Dusty would have none of it. His persistent whining brought Dave into the shed, who insisted that the boys fight fair. Their father would never tell them this, but he was impressed by their competitive spirit.

Poor Dave! Every year, the Hoedown has-beens set themselves for another beating, and every year, he ran the gauntlet between Annie and her creations and the lads and their billy carts. Now, Chloe added to the confusion, having entered Patricia in the "Cuddly Creatures" competition. Her mother was doing decorative duck eggs and didn't have time to attend to her normal responsibilities (e.g., meals, bed-making, washing, and ironing). Such is life.

These festivals inject much-needed dollars into the economy of a country town, and Dusty started it all by breaking the tape at the showgrounds to get the sheepdog trials underway. His relatives competed, which is why he couldn't be a judge for those events. Needless to say, he hung around as a keen observer of the "Best in Show" parade. Mimi, the sniffer dog from H.M. Customs, looked well-groomed and a beauty among beasts. The horny hound was a bit of a beast himself.

It wasn't necessary for security to patrol the main street, but the controlling canine liked to be sure all was going well. He would have been happy to see most shops doing brisk business, and the visitors lined up to meet him, having heard about the mongrel mayor. The dapper dandy didn't disappoint. With limited time available, Annie had run up a green waistcoat for him to wear, with a fancy M embossed on the side of the jacket.

You couldn't expect the little fella to run up and down the street all morning, so he picked a spot on the pavement outside Fat Al's and curled up for a kip, which didn't please the seagulls from Lake Disappointment, there for the French fries.

Lake Disappointment lapped languidly at the bottom of Harlequin Hill, near the Church of Praise, where baptisms used to take place at regular intervals. Sadly, the over-enthusiastic pastor drowned three babies during these ceremonies, and business was lost to the Roman Catholics, who maintained a depth limit on their baptismal font.

Over the school year, most of the youngsters in town attended the swimming academy on the lake, and this was fortuitous. Half the contestants in the billy cart race failed to handle Water Faucet Corner and plunged into the icy depths. All starters in the event were obliged to wear life vests.

The qualifying races continued throughout the afternoon, with a background noise of splashing and splintering as the choirmaster took his people through their last rehearsal in preparation for their evening performance. They sounded primed, pitch-perfect, and pleasing to the ear. The choirmaster exuded confidence, as did the vicar's wife, having placed a lobster ($20) on the boys and girls to bring home the bacon. At eight to one, this might have been an excellent bet but foolish and inadvisable. The previous Sunday, her husband rebuked those in his congregation who would even consider gambling.

The Church of Praise choir, scheduled to be the penultimate act, assembled by the side of the stage, dressed colourfully in their yellow and red smocks. Megan Proudfoot was in the throes of completing her performance, playing the Harp of Erin with her feet. In the judge's box, Dusty, with his head on Emmylou's lap, moaned quietly. The lady's magnified whisper defied the laws of unobtrusive discretion.

"Danny Boy must be turning over in his grave."

Everyone's a critic, aren't they? Diverse opinions give everybody a chance, exemplified by the raucous applause for Megan from Declan Murphy, who emerged from the pub, the worse for wear. Most of the church folks arrived to root for Bruce, with the expectation that he would lead the choir to a magnificent victory. The paedophile would have every opportunity to redeem himself in the eyes of the community. Many people thought "Nativity in Nashville" might win over these particular judges.

Those from other faiths were aware that the Church of Praise promoted a different interpretation of biblical history than conventional theology. The idea of the baby Jesus being born in Nashville received little support elsewhere; but, with a decent riff and a melodic chorus, hope springs eternal. The eight to one offered by the bookmakers was snapped up by those optimists with a sense of humour.

The optimists proved to be off the mark, although the COP choristers put on a brave show. New compositions are always up against it in competitions like this, whereas bastardisation seems to reign. "How Great Our Art," performed by first nation rock artists, won the contest, with the band members commended for being inclusive and non-confrontational. "A Ride with Me" was also commended, and school bus driver Melanie McGregor didn't seem offended by the false praise of Emmylou Paris.

"Very nice, Melanie, but don't give up your day job."

There would be no hard feelings between Bruce and Dusty. The animal's outstretched paw was accepted, and the former mayor acknowledged condolences from Keith and Emmylou. In retrospect, Mr Suburban may not have been as country as hoped.

THE BRUTES FROM BAKERSFIELD

It is not common to start a story at the end but it has been done before. One remembers the tearful funeral from *Chariots of Fire*, filmed in glorious Technicolor, with key scenes spiced with the evocative music of Vangelis. I suspect that my tantalising tale will not be adapted as a movie. I hope you don't think any less of me because of this.

One of my important characters is a small Shih Tzu called Pepe, who now resides in Chihuahua, Mexico. His return to California is temporary, as a witness in a murder trial in progress at Los Angeles Superior Court. Although not quite the end of the proceedings, things are not looking good for the Delmonico brothers, accused of gunning down a Native American in downtown LA. The hoodlums maintained that he was an alien from Planet Schloss.

You are correct. There is no such place as Planet Schloss. This is a bit of a yarn, so I suggest you get yourself a cup of coffee, and I will continue after the paragraph break.

Pepe is a familiar moniker, south of the border, also in California, where many Mexicans embrace this Spanish name for Joseph. Yes, the little tyke is a wetback, who swam the Rio Grande with his common-law carers, the Rodriguez family—Carlos and Carman and their two children, José and Juanita. The breadwinner hoped for a better life in America, and the kids, five and seven years, just went where their parents went. What other choice did they have?

Carlos, a mechanic, found work in New Mexico and Arizona on their way to California, where the couple opened a cantina in Bakersfield. The fellow, still surrounded by grease, etched out a living. Taco Tuesday proved to be a magnet for the local community, and what can one say about Fajita Friday? Margaritas of this size were a rarity this side of the border, and Happy Hour between 5.30 p.m. and 5.40 p.m. pulled in the punters. Quite a few itinerant workers lived in this area, including some ex-cons, who wouldn't be seen dead without a Tequila Slammer in their hand.

I am talking about the Delmonico brood. Who else? Luca and Rocco were immigrants from a village in Sicily called Corleone. Now, where have I heard that name before? This is what many of the other customers might have been saying, although the average Latino didn't bother with gangster films. Those with families would no doubt have taken their kids to Mickey Mouse or Snow White movies. The latter decision may have been based on envy, with racial discrimination rampant. Those from south of the border copped it from all quarters.

The two Italians must have acquired their street cred from Donald Duck. They were always under fire from those in rival gangs and other juvenile delinquents, envious of their quick rise up the greasy pole of petty larceny and other misdemeanours. The boys, hardly out of their teens, consolidated their reputation, and a future life of crime seemed assured. What were they like, you ask?

The courtroom was not the best place to harvest an accurate account of their true selves, as the prosecution's version painted them as young monsters, and the defence chose the misguided youth approach. Those in Bakersfield told a different story. The lads liked fast money, fast women, and fast food—all of these things attainable at Carman's Cantina. Sometimes the money aspect became a problem.

"Hey, Carlos, you are behind with our protection money. Do we have to crack a few bones to convince you of our support?"

This came from Rocco, in his best Vito Corleone impression. He could be quite imperious, especially when you consider that he resembled Danny DeVito more than the Sicilian gangster.

"I am sorry, Senor Delmonico, but it has been a bad month, and I 'ave been forced to let go kitchen staff. The times will be better soon. You 'ave patience, yes?"

Should the truth be known, Carlos employed no kitchen staff. Carman cooked most of the food, and the dog licked the plates clean before they went into the dishwasher. Considering all that, this was still the most popular diner around and open to everyone. The extortionists even became regular customers and often joshed with the other diners, including a few sassy street workers on their meal break.

Of the two lads, Luca claimed to be the intellectual, with his penchant for the arts. His favourite film, *The Texas Chain Saw*

Massacre, never disappointed. He didn't read books but was an ardent collector of comics. Did he regard himself as a modern-day superhero? Both siblings possessed a vivid imagination, and some of those Science Fiction stories were out of this world. Fancy all the inhabitants of Planet Schloss being albinos?

Little has been said about the murdered man because nobody knew where the bloody hell he came from. Most Indians in Los Angeles cited Mumbai or New Delhi as their home. The pundits from way back wallowed in their memories of a different age when Hollywood reached out for dark-skinned bodies to stock their Wild West movies. The folks on reservations near and far responded. The white man's money was good, with cigarettes and cigars freely available (everyone smoked in those days).

The film companies around Burbank churned out at least three Westerns per week, and box-office cowboys, from "Hoot" Gibson to John Wayne and Audie Murphy, shot redskins by the thousands. It was so difficult to maintain human resources that some studios used Australians as the typical Apache brave. Rock Hudson in war paint also performed a similar role in Winchester '73.

Questions needed to be asked:

"Was the victim an actor? In town to perform somewhere? Perhaps on television?"

The senior policeman, the first to arrive at the murder location, provided his opinion, which irked the medical examiner somewhat. Demarcation boundaries still exist, and this type of judgment should have been his prerogative.

"He's not acting. He's dead, all right."

The surrounding location in the immediate aftermath of a homicide can be a busy place. You have the ME, the investigators who always arrive late, the boys in blue who cordon off the area, and the media, if a high-profile person is involved. Would anyone notice the presence of a small dog, ever-present and engrossed in proceedings?

In another life, Pepe may have been an excellent gumshoe himself. The way he sniffed his way around the crime scene reeked of professionalism, and it wasn't just the food bins at the back of the Chinese chop house that demanded his attention. Detective Sergeant Kosky kept dogs of her own and always carried a treat in her pocket. Just pat his head and slip him a delicacy, and the world will be a better place.

When the life support vehicle arrived to transport the corpse away from the crime scene, the dog jumped aboard the LSV and refused to leave. The alert woman realised that the bow-wow and the Cherokee must have been an item, and the unkempt canine may have seen the brutal slaying.

With the ambulance on its way to the morgue for an autopsy, the high achiever from Homicide returned to her reflections and pondered on John Doe's identity. The poor guy had been stripped of valuables and ID documents, not that anyone expected to find a Diner's Club Gold Card on his person. However, a paper trail beside the body gave up miscellaneous bits and pieces, probably discarded by the thugs as items of no value. Sonja picked up one such item, a bus ticket stub for a journey that commenced in Bakersfield.

The medical examiner provided his verbal report that afternoon.

"Your JD is around forty-five years of age, a weathered face with a one-inch scar on his left cheek. Brown hair, ponytail style, and two of his teeth are missing; the rest are in reasonable condition. Of the four bullet wounds, one punctured his lung, another his abdomen, and two others severed multiple blood vessels. He bled out. His kidneys were in poor shape, not so his appetite. His last meal consisted of Menudo, Frijoles, Churros, rice, and corn tortillas."

The diet-conscious detective was a steak-and-no-fries kind of girl, but she appreciated the fact that this information gave them a better chance to track down the identity of John Doe. Could it be as simple as a Mexican restaurant in Bakersfield?

"A Mexican restaurant in Bakersfield!" repeated LAPD's most knowledgeable trencherman. Ricky Fingalos, overweight but never overwrought, was lucky to be working at all. To pass the physical in this precinct, you have to defeat a three-legged member of the K9 division over fifty yards. Because he lost, he ended up with a desk job. You would never see Ricky walking the beat, but as a connoisseur of eating establishments, hail the king.

"They say the food is exceptional at Carmen's, but the clientele is a bit seedy. I wouldn't flash my badge around, that's for sure."

Sonja reached her out-of-town destination at noon on a typical working day and reported to the local precinct, where she asked for assistance. Her temporary side-kick, a twenty-year-old greenhorn, had never been under a woman before, and experience is everything.

They reached the cantina within the hour and observed about fifteen diners wolfing down their vittles. The sergeant and her companion strode boldly to the counter and turned around to find only three people left. Did somebody ring the taco bell?

"Are you the owner of this establishment, sir?"

Senior sergeants always rely on their junior to get the ball rolling, and the lad did have jurisdiction qualifications. However, the dude with the spatula in his hand looked fearsome, and his response was rather rude. Sonja could be confrontational herself. She was no shrinking violet.

"What if I am, numbnuts, doesn't cut it Mr Carman, or whatever your name is. We're investigating a homicide, and if we need to close this joint and take you downtown, we will. Have you got that, sugarlips?"

Sugarlips didn't look Mexican, but the officers spied a woman in the kitchen with dark features. Perhaps she hadn't married well. If this was her husband, he had let himself go. The stubble around his chin must have been three days old, and Procter and Gamble would have salivated over the state of his apron. Bring on the Tide detergent.

After the initial confrontation, the surly smartass invited the two police officers to an empty table, and he took off his apron. They were grateful for that. His hostility waned, and he proved to be quite informative.

"My name is not Carmen. That was one of the previous owners. The diner became available after an unfortunate incident six months ago, which is when I purchased the eatery. I have murdered no one, but that doesn't mean I didn't want to."

At this time, little Miss Nosy wasn't interested in the incident. She just wanted someone to identify the deceased. They had canvassed film studios, cigar stores, and community centres but to no avail. A mystery man with a scar on his face shouldn't be so invisible. Albinos with dark skin are not easy to forget.

OK, I admit it. Some of my tales aren't high on the believability scale, but there were no reservations with this guy. The titan of the tamales recognised him, even though the picture proffered was his autopsy portrait.

"Hey, that's Pablo Big Buffalo. He looks great."

"I'm afraid to tell you that Mr Buffalo is no longer with us," said the no-nonsense policewoman, excited that she had tracked down a buddy. "Can you tell us what you know of the said gentleman, his circumstances, and his place of abode? Do you have that information Mr...?"

"Eggleston, Ham. You say he's dead. I can't believe it. The man was a saint. He even took over the Rodriguez dog when the family died. How did it happen?"

"Whoa, whoa, you first, amigo," exclaimed the woman with a lot of questions. "Rodriguez is a name I'm not familiar with."

Then it all came out. The previous owners, Carlos and Carman, were God's gift to humanity. They befriended their best customers and gave them small gifts on their birthdays and anniversaries. The Native American and Ham Eggleston were such friends and, to a lesser extent, the Delmonico brothers, even though they continued to extract protection money from the restaurateur. It's a strange world.

"You could call the Indian and the dog buddies, but Pablo didn't get on with the Italians; fortunately, they dined at different times. It didn't bother Carlos or Carman that their friend was an albino, but Luca and Rocca claimed he came from another sphere."

Ham didn't elaborate on that state of affairs. He wanted to describe the unfortunate incident and explain how he acquired the business as a going concern.

"The family always ate their meals in the kitchen. One day, a large pot of chilli sauce exploded, and all of them, including the kids, received severe burns and were rushed to Memorial Hospital on 34th Street. On this occasion, there would be no miracle on 34th Street.

Over the next few days, they all succumbed to their injuries. Carlos, the last to go, transferred ownership of the diner to me before he expired. I agreed for the purchase money to be paid in instalments to a trust for the welfare of the Shih Tzu, with Pablo as fund manager. He had experience with cash."

"He was an accountant," suggested the polite listener.

"Hell no," replied the hash jockey. "He was a croupier at one of those casinos we have in Kern County."

With a lot to take in, Sonja Kosky ploughed on. She wanted to know where Scarface resided and details of any next of kin. Eggleston provided all the answers.

"Naw, no relatives in this neck of the woods. The guy lived alone down the highway, by the Trading Post."

"I know it," said the junior officer, delighted to be able to contribute to the conversation. "The Trading Post is a monument to the "Old West"—a place where Chief Sitting Bill used to sit whenever he came to town. It's popular with tourists."

Having commenced his story, the proprietor opted for the long version and called for nourishment.

"Hey, Maria, let's have some tacos and a few Cokes."

With that, he stared into the eyes of his new best friend and proceeded to trot out all his troubles.

"It hasn't been easy since I took over this eatery. Cooking for two people never bothered Maria, but multiple diners—Yikes! Then the dog started pining for José and Juanita. The mutt bonded OK with Pablo, but young people seem to understand animals better than adults. I wonder what happened to the ankle-biter. The last I saw of him, he went to LA with the Indian."

Pepe

"Pepe is fine and in care, but we were unaware he had money, so perhaps we might upgrade his accommodation. I can tell you that we have the Delmonico brothers in custody. We believe they gunned down the fund manager."

"Son of a bitch," cried Ham Eggleston. "The assholes deserve what they get. They tried their protection bullshit on me, and I tossed 'em out; banned 'em for life. If you need someone to help bring them down, give me a call. The mongrels put a brick through my window. They also robbed the police lock-up, the cheeky ferals. Got away with firearms, uniforms, you name it."

Sonja had heard about the heist at the precinct without being surprised. Too many movies glorified criminals in stolen uniforms, with the fad taking off in real life. She was also aware that the bullets that killed Buffalo were police issue. Nevertheless, her current priority was to obtain more information about the victim, and the Trading Post seemed the best place to obtain it. The entrance to the hacienda-type dwelling didn't have a front door, so she walked right in.

One could appreciate why the famous Indian chief would want to "take a load off" when he came to town. Most people wouldn't stand for the chaotic mess that greeted visitors. Blankets, calico cloth, peace pipes, hides, pottery, chewing tobacco, and extraneous objects were scattered around the showroom with no apparent order or system. The open doorway invited the winds to deliver dust and dirt into the mix, and an overriding smell of stale liquor permeated the room. At first, the indigenous public relations man didn't want to divulge the whereabouts of Big Buffalo's residence. Then the walk-in confided that she was a distant relative of Will Rogers, another stand-up kind of guy, with Cherokee heritage.

Of course, Sonja's folks came from Scandinavia, but we need to keep this story moving along. She found herself outside the humble abode of the murdered man and pushed at the wooden door. Open sesame! With no security system, could the owner have been relying on the guard-dog reputation of the Tibetan Terrier?

There was evidence of cohabitation. Pepe might have enjoyed the run of the house, with his eating bowl in the kitchen, and the permanent hutch in the corner of the bedroom indicated premium sleeping arrangements. Sonja adjudged the four-room home to be unexpectedly neat, perhaps with the exception of the back porch. Animal playthings lay all over the place, and the old rocking chair had seen better days. Is this where Pablo sucked on his pipe and told hunting stories to his naive companion?

You may wonder what the snoop expected to find in a dead man's digs. Perhaps something that would indicate why the albino travelled to LA? That something would be found in the wastebasket.

The mail delivery had been opened and the contents retained, because there was nothing but the discarded envelope in the trash, with the sender's name and address printed on the flap—Comicazi Pictures, Los Angeles, California.

"Yes, I am the MD of Comicazi, also the producer, director, and casting supremo. We adapt comic book fantasy to the silver screen and specialize in Science Fiction."

The last three films Kadesh Katz produced proved to be dogs. Anyone will tell you that. On the chance that the female dick wasn't up to speed, the flim-flam man waxed lyrical.

"We liaise with the cartoonist to provide the most accurate depiction of their characterisations and spare no research to find the best actors to fill these roles. This is why we approached Mr Big Buffalo. We needed albinos to portray aliens from Planet Schloss.

"You're making a movie of 'that' comic?" spluttered the female dick. She questioned the Delmonico brothers for hours on end, and they bent her ear to distraction about the albino from Planet Schloss—the one they supposedly shot.

It is unusual for law enforcement to still be working on a case while the trial is in progress, but there had been a delay in proceedings, sanctioned by the judge. The investigator knew the lead prosecutor feared his chief witness would be a target, and jury tampering might also be a possibility. Sonja, already thinking about her date with a divorce lawyer on Saturday night, was keen to wrap this up as soon as possible. All she wanted from Kadesh Katz were the facts.

"So, Mr Katz, can you confirm Mr Big Buffalo made contact with you regarding his participation in your film?"

"Damn right, he did. We offered him above award rates, and he demanded a part for the dog. Can you believe that?"

"Do they not have dogs on Schloss?" queried the now interested interrogator. "I read a book called *The Replicants*, and they had dishlickers on Planet Schmoo."

21

It appears that Pablo left the Comicazi premises without a deal, even though Katz agreed to review the script and consider the possibility of change. In Sonja's mind, the movie mogul was not a suspect. He would have killed the canine.

I suppose you are wondering why the woman is looking at an alternative perp because the killers confessed. Didn't they?

These kinds of admissions are grist to the mill for professional couch doctors, so the defence retained a shrink to comment on the mental stability of Luca and Rocco. Why waste money on a psychiatrist? Anyone could tell they were both whacko, so what price was their confession? These bozos just love notoriety.

Talking of love, her date advised Sonja that he intended to take her to a trendy new restaurant called Damian's in the Arts District. The authentic Mexican menu had tongues wagging, and it was just down the road from the scene of the crime.

It turned out that the guy wasn't a divorce lawyer but a divorced lawyer. There is a difference if you've been married three times. The only consolation for the professional policewoman was the possibility of going for a romantic after-dinner stroll to show her date where blood had been spilt.

The barricade tape was long gone, but the low life still lingered. She recognised half the itinerants as muggers and the other half were packing. The bachelor girl reached into her vest and removed her Saturday Night Special as a deterrent. Smith and Wesson like a walk on the wild side as much as anybody.

Also enjoying his weekend was the pooch without a partner. Having confirmed his healthy financial position, the logistics guru in the District Attorney's Office transferred the mutt into the honeymoon suite at the pet-friendly E-Central Hotel; half of the advisory group moved in with him. Someone needed to order room service.

The trial lawyer anticipated a difficult task ahead. Prepping a witness is always challenging, but asking a heartbroken animal to communicate with twelve good men and true is a challenge that only a confident attorney would embrace. The jurors would make their decision without fear or favour.

"He's a dog, for God's sake," said the most pessimistic of the team. "How is he going to bond with the jury?"

Mason Perry, the chief counsel, guessed that at least half the jurors kept pets. Man's best friend witnessed the crime; his own master was shot dead. He would react when he recognised the perpetrators of this foul act. Those in the big box would know whether the boys from Bakersfield did it or not.

The trial of the Delmonico brothers created curiosity right across the country. Even with a moratorium in place, the bookmakers in Las Vegas offered evens for the Electric Chair and two to one for Life. No one was betting on a not-guilty verdict. The prosecution team, confident and assured, would only put two witnesses on the stand: Pepe Rodriguez and the first responder, Officer Troy Pitt. The opposition argued among themselves as to whether they should subject their clients to any form of cross-examination. Once the boys started talking about Planet Schloss, the jury foreman could start rehearsing his one-word speech.

Sonja claimed a seat in the general court, with a clear view of the accused, sitting quietly beside their attorney. They appeared to enjoy being the focus of attention and occasionally waved to supporters in the public gallery. When I say supporters, they might have been relatives, but who would admit to that fact?

The dog was going to be the first to be called to the stand, and adjustments were made to accommodate him. With a little coaxing, he managed to paw the bible and provide his version of the affirmation oath, a discernible whine. A handler stood by, holding his lead, as Pepe stood up and scanned the extremities of the courtroom. The prosecutor took a backward step in disbelief. The little guy showed no interest in the people at the defence table, and only a passing interest in the jury; he gave them a dismissive growl.

"Is your name Pepe? Were you familiar with Pablo Bill Buffalo?"

Hearing a name he recognised, the dog responded, as you might expect, with an elongated whine of despair. The prosecutor continued.

"Were you with said individual on the night of July 9th last year, in downtown Los Angeles?"

Another whine of despair!

"Did you observe Rocco Delmonico or Luca Delmonico shoot your carer and best friend? Please bark into the microphone."

How embarrassing! The dog just eyeballed the judge impassively, stepped down from his position, and dragged his handler away to stymie further interrogation. Those in the general courtroom burst out laughing, as did those representing the accused. Mason Perry had been humiliated.

Not wanting to prolong his pain, prosecutor Perry called his next witness, Troy Pitt, who arrived, dressed in uniform and carrying a sidearm (which should have been lodged with one of the marshals). Pitt's arrival coincided with Pepe's departure; well, not quite.

The reticent hound and his lady-friend were about to depart through a side door when Pepe slipped his lead and rushed back into the well of the courtroom, barking like a dog possessed. He leapt at the policeman and tried to savage him. Pitt fended him off but the little beast kept coming at him. In a natural reaction, the man from the LAPD went for his gun, and, for a while, things didn't look great for poor Pepe.

Thank God for Angie, who was left holding the empty leash. She threw herself at the cop, disarmed him, and gave him one in the chops for good measure. What a brave, selfless act! She could have been killed. In the short time they had been together, the dog and his handler had become quite close. Pets tend to make friends easily, don't they?

The judge, horrified at this turn of events, called for calm. The gavel fell, the animal was evicted, and, after a break for medical treatment, Troy Pitt entered the witness box to be harangued and harassed by the defence counsel.

No, he had never seen the dog before and never set eyes on the deceased before the night of the slaying. Did he appear to be nervous? Absolutely!

On the back of recent developments, the beak agreed to another adjournment, and Sergeant Kosky was tasked with cleaning up the case. "Bull" Pitt would be held in protective custody based on his contempt of court (carrying a firearm). It turned out he couldn't afford bail.

Sonja flashed Pitt's picture around the casino where the victim worked, an obvious thing to do. The policeman was recognised and vilified. Over time, the fellow made multiple complaints against the croupier who had taken all his money from him—Pablo Bill Buffalo. The serving officer, now dirt-poor, blamed one man for his misfortune. By coincidence, he ran into that person on an unlit street corner, one black night in July. His mistake would be to call in the shooting; otherwise, he would not have needed to appear under oath.

One rarely appears as a witness for the prosecution on two separate occasions, but the four-legged fireball fronted up before the same judge, and his fine whining convinced everyone that Pitt was the perp. Yes, Luca and Rocco had been in the vicinity but were busy mugging a little old lady not more than a block away.

For those in the district attorney's office, there would be a small celebration in one of the local bars, where one of the ADAs praised and castigated the LAPD, whose servants partied elsewhere (the casino).

With reluctance, the strategy group moved out of their luxury accommodation, but Pepe would stay on with Angie before he returned to Chihuahua the following day. She ordered a pizza, and they watched a video of *Lady and the Tramp*.

THE BAD BOY FROM ILLINOIS

The reporter wanted to know why I was home alone. I could have admitted to irreconcilable differences, but I wasn't going to tell him that. I lied.

"My wife has gone to the Caribbean on holiday."

"Jamaica?" he guessed.

"No, she went of her own accord, but I will be joining her when I recover my passport from the authorities. There have been administrative problems."

I harboured no desire to tell him that my release from jail depended on me handing in my passport. Or that my wife left me because I shot the dog.

My so-called better half is a compassionate woman, and didn't view the incident as I did. Sure, I was out of it when I fired on the poor fella, but we've got another dog, so I don't see the problem.

I know you're wondering why the fourth estate would want to interview me. It isn't as if I am a high-profile personality or a reality TV star. Yes, over the years, my name has often been mentioned concerning several unsolved murders in the Chicago area, but that's what happens when you acquire a reputation. In truth, I should be more worried about the people from Inland Revenue. Just as Al Capone claimed to be a hard-working furniture dealer, I promote myself as a new-age influencer.

You will not find my website on the internet. My instrument of influence is a Ruger 38 Special Revolver, but down in the cellar, you will discover a collection of pump action shotguns, repeater rifles, knuckle-dusters and hunting knives. The Boy Scout organisation always maintained that you should be prepared.

The invitation to be the keynote speaker at the Temperance Society on St. Patrick's Day came as a surprise. My daughter may have been behind the nomination, as she knows what I get up to on Paddy's day. It must have been the ridiculous nature of the engagement that created interest in the media. The reporter on my doorstep looked inexperienced, but he had boned up on my rap sheet and living arrangements. The kid knew we kept woofers.

"I recall, Mr O'Flaherty, you owned two beautiful Afghan hounds. Did I not see them on the cover of *Playmate*, last year?"

"You did, young man. Ben and Bessy were "Playmate Pets" in the May edition. You're a dog owner yourself?"

Steve Kent lived with budgerigars, but admitting this fact would not give him the leverage he needed to appeal to such a prickly person. For this interview, he borrowed a co-worker's Irish setter, who proceeded to thrash around in his car while Steve knocked on Mr O'Flaherty's door. The repairs to his upholstery would set him back at least $400.

"I am an animal lover, sir. Which is why I was so disappointed to discover you shot your dog."

I have to admit I overreacted with that young journalist. However, I did send flowers to his hospital ward, and it was gratifying to learn that he would be able to consume solid food in four or five weeks. Because of this altercation and the unfortunate accident with Ben, ASPCA came at me with all guns blazing. The do-gooders also had my wife in their corner, didn't they? Just because I killed poor Benny, they seemed to think I failed the test as a fit and proper person to care for a pet. Can you believe the misery moll wanted custody of Bessy? Geeezus! The bitch doesn't even know where her bones are buried (I'm not talking about the dog).

It is accepted that I am a bit of a tough nut, but ASPCA people have no fear. In this instance, the field officer brought along a Rottweiler for company, but he should have insisted on a female for backup. As soon as the jet-black German locked eyes on the beautiful Afghan, it was love at first sight.

Now, I'm as randy as the next person, but this Romeo wouldn't take no for an answer, which embarrassed his master. Richard Head transformed from an assertive, domineering plaintiff to a snivelling, pathetic party pooper. He regained control of the animal's lead but only reduced the dog's impetus marginally. What a shame about our set of Waterford Crystal glasses, and the 19th-century porcelain vase was one of my wife's favourites.

"Thanks for calling, Richard. Should I send the breakage invoice to head office?"

The above ramblings of Terry O'Flaherty, of no fixed employment, were transcripts taken from an authorised recording device operated by licensed psychiatrist Rufus Okay. R.U. Okay, a court-appointed professional, had been engaged to verify or deny Mr O'Flaherty's claim of mental impairment. If deemed a felony, TOF's cruel act might get him five years of jail time. Should the shrink make the wrong judgement, it could earn him some concrete shoes and a boat ride on Lake Michigan. Most of the gangster's friends knew he was as mad as a cut snake.

Steve Kent, although knocked up pretty badly, managed to file his story, and the headline didn't look good for the bad boy from Illinois.

"TERRY O'FLAHERTY SHOOTS HIS DOG."

It needs to be said that the gentleman in the black shirt and white tie was no stranger to publicity. For those TikTok misfits, unfamiliar with prose, I can report that TOF might well be the darling of the Chicago underworld. Most folks might have been shocked by all his crimes and misdemeanours, but they loved reading about them.

Many people are fascinated by the way others live, and no intrusion is too unreasonable. The Afghans became exposed to the public eye on many occasions, due to their centrefold appearance in *Playmate*. You may be surprised to learn that TOF's first choice for a favourite friend was a poodle, but Ben and Bessy arrived as payment for a debt. The two dogs then proceeded to eat everything in sight, and all that preening and pampering must have frustrated Terry. Fortunately, the wife proved to be a great help before her departure to the Caribbean.

Yes, the big lie was back on the table. No one had laid eyes on the ever-suffering woman for some days, and her sister hadn't heard from her. A visitor to the O'Flaherty residence spied wet galoshes on his back porch. Had someone been out on Lake Michigan?

Bernadette Brennan was no fan of the law and would not be waiting for her sister's "missing" file to become a cold case. Bernie lived in a rather upmarket retirement village, and one of her constant companions in the Bingo hall was retired discount detective Paddy Pest.

Patrick Pesticide, an Australian, acquired a Green Card by virtue of his sleuthing on behalf of the president. Yes, the man turned out to be a national hero, but he didn't advertise the fact, although he would have liked to. He just couldn't remember anything much past breakfast.

With such a reputation, he had to be the right man to investigate the asshole from Arlington Heights, who married Kay Brennan, despite opposition from her family and fellow members of her book club. One of those family members spelt it out for the former detective.

"Paddy, you've read the newspapers. If this clown could shoot his dog, what might he do to his wife? Kay isn't easy to live with."

"I hear what you say, Bernie. How long has she been gone? Is her cell phone also missing?"

In this day and age, a mobile phone is like a third arm for everybody and, in Kay's case, rarely silent. She would ring friends and relations at least twice a day. Sometimes, she called her husband, who resided in a different bedroom.

People reading this epistle might question why anyone in their right mind would turn to a burnt-out crime-fighter with concentration issues. During his career, Pest relied on the resources of certified hornbag Stormy Weathers. Stormy always had his back (and front) and saved him from embarrassing situations on many occasions. Bernadette the Bold was asking him to put his life on the line against a mean Chicago hombre. In the spirit of Maxwell Smart, he would do it and tell everyone he was loving it.

"Good evening, Mr O'Flaherty. My name is Patrick Pesticide, and I'm here to talk about your wife. Can I come in?"

O'Flaherty had been gone from Ireland many years, but he seemed to recall some Pesticides from the bogs around Kilkenny. This guy spoke with an accent he didn't recognise.

Best to humour him, thought the wary host.

"Take a seat, Patrick. Would you like a drop of Bushmills? You can't beat a single malt in this weather."

It was cold alright, but the frozen investigator would not get near the fireplace with the dog already there. For a moment, the hairy hound may have seen the visitor as a threat, but she just stifled a growl and lay back on the white wool rug. O'Flaherty produced the whiskey and manufactured his most accommodating smile. People who see this smile don't often live to tell the tale.

If there was one problem, it would be Paddy and the animal kingdom. The man didn't like dogs, cats, spiders, snakes and bears, and these are the types of creatures that smell fear in a human. However, Bessy, the

Afghan, didn't look unlike his uncle Shamus, almost ninety-three. They got on quite well.

"Nice dog. I read you shot him. Don't tell me the press are exaggerating again."

This opening salvo from the distinguished dick was skilfully presented. He was aware the man hated the media, and this approach might get him onside with the thug.

"They were writing about her brother. Bessy didn't care much. Now there's more room in front of the fire for her."

Pest asked all the difficult questions but to no avail. At one stage, the animal attempted to sit up but then changed her mind and returned to the floor with a yawn, possibly a demonstration of disdain aimed at the visitor. If Paddy thought so, he didn't say anything. One doesn't want to advertise paranoia. Nevertheless, the dog didn't stand up when he took his leave. Obedience training is not what it used to be nor is general hospitality. Terry O'Flaherty failed to offer him another whiskey, and his smile seemed artificial. The pensioner expected Bernie to demand all the facts.

"So, Paddy, how did it go with the dog killer?"

Bernadette was impressed he got to first base with the mobster, but there were no answers regarding the disappearance of her sister or the missing phone. She had been ringing her number and reading the death notices, even though she should have been the first to know. There are over two and a half million funerals in the USA every year, and many of them in Illinois. Industry speak for a coffin is a "Chicago raincoat." The murder rate in this city is four times the national average.

Pest had a plan. He explained to his lady friend that the visit to Chez O'Flaherty should be regarded as a journey of reconnaissance. The man seemed to be holding back because you don't give top-shelf Irish whiskey to a walk-in unless you've got something to hide. The weak link might be the Afghan. What Paddy wanted to do was bold and fraught with danger.

"I think we ought to kidnap the dog."

The response to this suggestion was measured but absolute—a reply first attributable to Nelson Bridwell of Lone Ranger and Tonto fame.

"What do you mean 'we' white man?"

"Hell, Bernie, someone's got to drive the getaway car. I'll have my hands full with the foo foo. Do you want to see your sister again or what?"

31

Some people can be persuasive, and the Wonder from Down Under was always candid with his comments. Bernadette considered her options, as Mr Blunt explained his inspired plan.

"We know the guy is an after-hours person. While he is doing the rounds at his favourite nightspots, we break into his house with a syringe and a sirloin. The mutt won't know what day it is. Believe me, the dog-napping will be easy. Getting the pooch to take us to your sister will be another thing. Do you have any items of Kay's clothing that she can sniff? If not, we can raid the closet in her bedroom."

Paddy and Stormy once had sex in a closet while staking out the living quarters of a female serial killer, so he felt comfortable with women's clothes. If the scent took Bessy back home to find her mistress, there would be a case for digging up the hoodlum's back garden. Of course, he didn't share this scenario with his fragile friend.

The deterrent for illegal entry never seems to bother private investigators, and this one would be no different. The O'Flaherty residence didn't boast security cameras, but the canny home-owner had placed hidden touchpads underneath each of his downstairs windows. If you stepped on one, you were subjected to the gruesome growl of a South American gorilla, a powerful warning for would-be burglars.

I'm not going to tell you how I know this or why the kidnappers chose to go through the front door. Only kidding! Paddy possessed one of those keyrings most robbers would die for, and outsmarting an Irishman didn't seem that hard, notwithstanding the fact he was half-Irish himself.

Once inside, they disabled Alarm System 1. Alarm System 2 was asleep by the fireplace, but the smell of sirloin woke the forever-hungry animal seconds before Doctor Pesticide plunged the syringe into his hairy torso. Leaving Bernie to carry the comatose beast out to the car, the fearless one ascended the winding staircase in search of the lady's bedroom.

When the reluctant intruder returned to the house, she found her companion in the boudoir, staring at the depository of designer delights. No sooner had she entered the doorway when the questions started coming.

"Can you give me a description of your sister?" asked Paddy, while absorbing the contents of the wardrobe.

"Sure. She's your typical average socialite—bleached blonde hair, 11 stone, 5 feet 5 inches, erect, hard-nosed, and she has a tongue like a lizard with a lisp."

"So, she's not Chinese."

"Of course she's not Chinese," said the confused conspirator as she rushed across the room to see what was in the closet.

There in front of her, she observed a small Asian woman with a tennis ball in her mouth and a knife in her belly.

"Oh my God," shouted the shocked senorita.

As usual, Pest proved to be unflappable and provided an opinion that the body was a few days dead. He didn't want to mess with any evidence, so he slipped one of the gowns off its hanger and departed the scene with his accomplice. His subsequent 911 call, disguised and muffled, would be logged as anonymous.

The next day, Paddy took breakfast with his hairy friend, who no doubt remembered him from the gumshoe's earlier visit to her master's abode. The night shift at *The Tribune* had been adept and resourceful because the morning headline indicated that media leaks were still the order of the day at police headquarters:

"DID TERRY O'FLAHERTY KILL HIS COOK?"
Missing Afghan Sought by Police.

Over at the Afghanistan embassy, the PR department moved into damage control. How could this rag of a newspaper insinuate a human from their country might be responsible for this foul act? "A lie by omission," screamed the ambassador, demanding an explanation. By then, the editor-in-chief was puffing on his cigar and evaluating the circulation figures, which always increased when gangsters were involved.

Vital information that didn't find itself in the public arena was the fact that Kay O'Flaherty's fingerprints were found on the murder weapon, hardly unexpected, the weapon being a kitchen knife. To tell the truth, Terry would have a hard time remembering where his kitchen was. He was not the kind of husband who helped with the dishes.

Bernadette Brennan wasn't the kind of sister who scared easily, but all this publicity spooked her. If the sniffer dog chose to return to his domain, there would be a welcoming committee dressed in blue. Paddy had other ideas.

"Let's try the waterfront first. I know this is not what you want to hear, and the odour of fish might counteract the aroma of a Prada playsuit, but O'Flaherty does have a boat registered in his name. If Kay has been on it, we'll find out."

Dave Kelly had never been in the navy, but he called himself a commodore; the deception proved beneficial for his charter business. Actually, not really his business. Terry O'Flaherty owned the vessel and supplied him with quite a few customers, destined for the deep. Return trips were rare.

The Afghan recognised the salty old sailor and ran up to him, expecting a treat. No luck there, so she jumped onto the deck of the mid-sized craft and headed for the galley. Paddy would have been hoping the animal wouldn't lose sight of her mission—to find evidence that Kay had been aboard recently.

The grumpy seafarer spewed out his bile.

"Who are you, and what are you doing with Bessy? The police are looking for this dog."

"Indeed they are, sir. And they may also have you under surveillance. Some people say this vessel is always carrying ice, even in winter. Would you like to provide a comment, my friend?"

Wow! Was it Henry Kissinger who said, "The most daring course is often the safest?" Did he ever go to Chicago?

Kelly and Pest were standing on the pier, and if the aforementioned gentleman were to swing those ropes he carried, Paddy would have got his bottom wet. The sound of a horn eased the tension, and our man stepped back to relative safety. The dog reappeared and bounded off to liaise with Bernadette in the car. The Aussie chancer followed, not wanting to look back, sure that Mr Kelly would be reaching for his cell phone. He was not wrong.

Bernie was relieved her sister's scent wasn't found aboard M.V. Eternity. Kay was feisty and not short of a word, but she would be up against it if confronted by the cantankerous commodore. The bald man with the "Popeye" tattoo would not be able to put a name to the inquisitive stranger, but his boss would recognise the description immediately.

Time to return the dog home, thought Paddy. We'll do it in the morning.

"Let's drop her off around the corner and then drive past the residence," said the determined detective, as he gunned his vehicle up to fifty miles per hour. These days, thrills were few and far between. When urged, Bessy jumped out of the car and bounded off in the direction of her favoured fireplace. The senior sleuths continued along the boulevard of bad taste, with Bernie forever vigilant.

"Oh my God!" she cried, this phase fast becoming her favourite expression.

"The man tending O'Flaherty's garden—it's Commodore Kelly."

"He's probably on a retainer," said Paddy, proving to be a consummate know-all. "In big business, they are called personal assistants. I bet he's also a bodyguard."

If Mr Pest knew all the facts, the bets would be off. He later discovered the gentleman in question had been married to the cook, not that her demise affected his daily grind in any way. Chores were chores. Am I right?

A criminal analyst will tell you that the first stage of a murder investigation is finding a motive. If the victim is a chef, the motive is obvious, but Mrs Kelly, a native of Hong Kong, boasted few critics. Terry liked Chinese food, and so did his wife. As far as American chow was concerned, May churned out a half-decent hamburger, but suspicions lingered regarding her hot dogs.

In the old days, Paddy always maintained a contact at police headquarters, making information easy to come by. Now, he relied on the *Chicago Tribune*, and they rarely disappointed. The current thinking indicated TOF was having a quiet night at home, reading the latest Salman Rushdie novel, with Ella Fitzgerald belting it out in the background. May delivered his meal on a tray, but it didn't live up to expectations. Later, he lurched into the kitchen with stomach cramps. There followed a shouting match, and the famous O'Flaherty temper came to the fore. A knife was produced.

Salman, Ella, and anyone else with an opinion might well appreciate the possibility of such a scenario, but why would he carry her upstairs to his wife's closet? As for the tennis ball, she didn't play tennis.

There proved to be alternative thinking—from those who saw Kay O'Flaherty as the killer, presently nowhere to be seen. Her fingerprints were on the murder weapon, and the lady was spotted arguing with Dave Kelly on the foreshore. Needless to say, the sailor with the green fingers was also mentioned in despatches. The husband is always a suspect.

The break in the case appeared on Friday 13 December. How lucky for the police that a member of the public handed in a wallet to the local precinct, a Christmas present for them. It belonged to Terry O'Flaherty, who didn't report his cash or house key missing. Ho, ho, ho and ha, ha, ha, somebody forgot to lock their car.

When interviewed, the glib victim claimed his property was stolen during his address at the temperance function. Fingerprints lifted from the leather wallet implicated one Raphael Dahl, former juvenile delinquent and pick-pocket, now a tennis professional, who dispensed lessons to the sons and daughters of the rich and famous. I hate to bring too many animals into this story, but the man was also an efficient cat burglar.

I know what you're thinking— a tennis ball in the victim's mouth, and so on. It has to be him. Well, that's what the boys in blue said, but proving the obvious is another thing. In the subcontinent, dahl is a spiced curry, so there's your double play. Was May's experimentation with Indian food unauthorised? Perhaps Raphael was a hitman from Hyderabad?

This is the kind of tale I might have put together if Pest had been a little younger (and owned a faster car). Right here, right now, the fuzz were doing their job. Paddy's commitment was to find Bernadette's sister. Nothing more. Nothing less.

In the end, this turned out to be a far more puzzling situation than the obvious murder. Everybody understands the Chicago Police Department doesn't condone violence among their own. However, in this case, they beat the crap out of Dahl, and he confessed. He also accompanied a small force to the O'Flaherty house to relive the sad event, which I have recorded as follows:

The accused possessed a key, so he went through the front door and experienced no trouble with the alarm, disarmed during the day. He dressed in tennis gear, carrying his racquet, balls, and a sports bag for the jewels. The kitchen was empty, so he grabbed a knife from the block on his way to the staircase, the only sound being an animal snoring.

Upstairs, he crept into Kay's boudoir, not knowing that May was also heading in the same direction. With the lady of the house away, little Miss Envious was going to sample her very expensive Poison perfume.

It is not uncommon to find a man in a woman's bedroom, but even Roger Federer wouldn't rifle a lady's underwear drawer. The cook opened her mouth to scream, and in went the tennis ball, quickly followed by the knife to the stomach. Dahl explained that he didn't want to stab her. It was just instinctive.

Of course, it was. Just as it would be instinctive of the judge to send him down for life. Having completed the re-enactment, Raphael may have made a similar assessment because, instead of joining the others by the bedroom door, he ran to the open window and jumped from the second floor onto the pavement below. He landed head first on one of the pressure patches, and one and all trembled to the gruesome howl of a South American gorilla. The frightening noise even woke Bessy up.

Did anyone feel sympathy for Terry? With his wife, the former actress, missing, there would be no ham this year, and the dog would have no canine company.

"You can't hide the facts, Bessy," said Terry, feeling sorry for himself. In the aftermath of recent events, he now conversed with the pet regularly.

"It's Christmas and we are going to be all alone, with no one to cook our food. Would you like a small nip of the Bushmills?" TOF, now drinking from the neck of the bottle, routinely sloshed a little of the firewater into the dog's bowl. Bessy was starting to get a taste for it.

Dave Kelly advised his boss that the house would hold dark memories for some time to come, and he would be spending the holidays on the vessel. The gardening commodore had taken two geranium pots along for company. The good news for Bernadette came a few days after Christmas with a call from her sister.

"Could you collect me from O'Hare International?" Paddy cranked up the vehicle and they arrived at the designated terminal an hour early. That's how keen they were.

What a sight—Kay O'Flaherty with the best suntan in Chicago! How healthy the woman looked, wearing a colourful summer dress, and she almost glided into view in her flip-flops, carrying presents for everyone. The burning question would be, "Where had she been?" Not before Bernadette could comment on her attractive casual outfit.

"Gee, sis, this is how they dress in Jamaica."

A FORK IN THE ROAD

When you meet Sophie for the first time, one is immediately impressed by her convivial nature and natural beauty. That sweet face is something to behold and she is particularly well-groomed for a gal of tender years. Her bright eyes continually shine in permanent anticipation, always hoping for the arrival of a new experience. Yes, she has loose lips and a cold nose, but you would expect that from a three-year-old Labrador.

Was Sophie special? Of course, she was. Being a family dog shouldn't denigrate her standing in the canine world. Sure, Benji and Old Yeller became high achievers, and some mutts could do tricks (I say that in the nicest possible way), but this energetic hound presented as intelligent, friendly, and nice to be around. Exuding charisma and charm, she consistently won over the sharpest critics, and because of Sophie's importance to the household, many unfortunate incidents were overlooked.

"Bad dog. You just crapped in Daddy's slippers."

Chastisement proved a rarity. It is not surprising our girl took advantage of this situation. Wouldn't you?

Sophie

The Shanahans resided at Farm Hill, less than a mile out of town, on an unmade road, pot-holed and precarious. Their unpretentious home accommodated Dan, Doris, Aunt Daisy, and the three kids, Dorothy, David, and Dolores.

The pampered pet lived on the verandah in a purpose-built doghouse. The store-bought, single-entrance, faux-timber unit had been colourfully painted and boasted the usual living necessities: a flat cushion, superfluous to family needs; a hand-woven blanket from the Doris hippie era; and two bowls for daily sustenance. Certain collectables were transported in and out of the dog box at will. These included Mr Shanahan's left foot dress shoe, gone missing after a golf club soiree, plus one of David's rubber robots from his Star Wars collection. This latter item was sometimes discovered in the homeowner's habitat at the other end of the porch.

Dan's temporary sleeping quarters (Doghouse 2) were bigger than Sophie's but just as basic. The itinerant visitor would see a camp stretcher on the deck with a pillow and a couple of blankets piled on the canvas mattress. The man of the house readily admitted to spending too much time at the golf club, and Doris knew when to lock the door and banish him from the conjugal bed.

"You're two hours late for dinner, and you smell like a brewery. Go to bed, keep quiet, and don't bother the dog."

In truth, the panting pet enjoyed the company and often relocated to the other kennel, where Dan's snoring seemed like a symphony of solidarity. Although the situation with the slippers remained a sore point, they were still friends.

It is hard to know when the exasperated woman first contemplated killing her husband. One needs to think these things through. The kids still attended school, and the loss of the breadwinner's income would be a setback. Then again, the unmarried Fred Farnsworth from the funeral parlour seemed obsessed with the homely but still attractive housewife—the homely housewife, once apprenticed to her father, the town butcher. Could the aforementioned Fred come under consideration regarding the disposal of a body?

Sophie, through no fault of her own, became an eyewitness to the lady's evil considerations, when she rested her weary bones on her lap as her mistress flicked through the *New York Times* best-seller *Hard to Detect Poisons*. In no way did this make her an accessory before the fact, but one must consider the demarcation line. In the dog world, allegiance is always given to those who feed you, and Doris replenished the food bowl at regular intervals. It must be said that Dan paid for all those vet visits, but the dog didn't like the vet much, so the male mentor lost valuable Brownie points, irrespective of those late-night bonding sessions on the verandah.

Also vying for the animal's affection were the little people, who declared her an honorary human, thus requiring her to commit to humanoid pastimes such as running, jumping and playing fetch. No wonder the active animal appeared so weary at the end of the day. Membership of the fan club didn't include Aunt Daisy. Jumping at her was fraught with danger and left one open to consequences. Sophie once received the backside of a frying pan for her trouble.

The question should be asked—"Did Doris ever love Dan?" The answer is "Yes." They married in a fever (thank you, Johnny Cash) and lived the first few years in marital bliss. D's dad paid his daughter a generous stipend at the butcher shop, and her beloved sold bad cars to good people. Believe it or not, the town folk never blamed him when their vehicle gave up the ghost two weeks after the warranty expired. All the same, he avoided these individuals at the pub and socialised at the golf club. Nobody there ever bought a vehicle from the scoundrel and was not likely to.

Given his marketing skills in the used car lot, one would be surprised to learn that the fellow didn't maintain this confidence at home, always seeking reassurance from his wife regarding the state of their marriage. Those "I love ya, honey, but the dog comes first." pledges became less frequent, and once the third child arrived, they dried up completely. One evening he retired for the night and found the hound languishing in his bed space. Right there, right then, he should have realised the gig was up and checked for meat cleavers in the kitchen.

There has always been much discussion regarding pets in the bedroom because some animals tend to drool a bit. This is not a bodily function precipitated by any emotional craving, which is the *Homo sapiens* experience. It's hard to be a cobber if you slobber, so Sophie learnt about Listerine and accepted the application of a dog deodorant that Doris applied daily. The woman still slept with a warm body but one that didn't exhale alcohol fumes.

At the pre-trial inquest, it would not be definitively determined that the wife skewered her husband with that three-pronged pitchfork, but her fingerprints were on the weapon. Nevertheless, this didn't exonerate

Aunt Daisy and the kids from consideration, all having motives, especially the youngsters. Dan imposed unreasonable limitations on their screen time, including *Sesame Street* and *The Simpsons*, and when he refused to put his hand in his pocket for that Wiggles concert, this didn't go down well at all.

Inquisitive folks questioned the presence of a pitchfork on the property in the first place. The pitchfork belonged to Jude Ashbury, the feed merchant. Known to all as Hay Jude, the chap often delivered bales to the back paddock for Pony Club, which Mrs Shanahan supervised every Sunday. Leaving this tool behind on that seditious Sunday may have been a great temptation to someone.

After the inquest came the trial, which is what happens when they arrest someone. Quite frankly, Doris didn't think the murder rap would stick, as the best lawyer in town would appear in her corner. Unfortunately, the DPP appointed the best lawyer out of town, and Haydn Collingwood proved to be a beast that not only pried, prodded and parried, but his persistent probes were particularly personal, including the relationship between Doris and Fred Farnsworth, and what they did in the coffin room. What they did in the coffin room shocked the God-fearing, conservative community beyond belief.

Because of these revelations, public support for the locked-up lady disappeared, and she received few visitors in the clink. One frequent caller, however, was Sophie the Steadfast. As her mistress wasted away in Stoney Lonesome, the poor thing wasted away at the farmhouse. With no one feeding her, the laconic Labrador lost quite a bit of body fat, which gave her the ability to sneak through the bars at the country jail and comfort her ladyship. The desk sergeant didn't mind and even shared his doughnut with the devoted dishlicker.

With Dan dead and Doris in detention, Daisy became Director of Discipline at Chez Shanahan—no easy ride. These kids could be unpredictable and hard to catch when given their head. Have you ever tried to herd cats? Another difficult problem involved providing answers to their questions.

"When is our mum coming home?" said Dorothy.

"Did mummy kill daddy?" asked Dolores.

"Can we watch *Play School*?" enquired David.

Daisy wasn't your traditional granny, who doted on the pubescent post-millennials. She usurped this position, as the real grandparents gave the little monsters a wide berth. Being Doris' sister, it would be incumbent on her to assist in any way as compensation for her free board and lodging. Then there was the apprehended violence order hanging over her head. Sis provided some measure of stability with the guarantee of a fixed address, but a further transgression might be awkward. If the children had been aware of Daisy's turbulent and unruly past, they might have made her a role model.

OK, I understand. Explanation needed.

First of all—the kids! Yes, they were monsters, and Dolores was the worst. One remembers the small carpet snake she slipped into her gran's handbag, which brought on heart palpitations and an ambulance trip to the hospital. Dorothy collected maggots and kept them in a large container under the house. When someone she didn't like accepted a dinner invitation, she released a bunch of the critters into the visitor's soup. After that, guests became very nervous when they saw Dot on waitressing duties. David's primary target was his father, who refused to sanction the purchase of those tickets for the Wiggles concert. The little pest glued two of Dan's golf clubs together.

Daisy had also been a wild child and not one to be swept off her feet by a used car salesman with a degree in deception. Her peers rode motorbikes and were always persons of interest to the gendarmes in many municipalities. This new-age woman wore leather and could kick ass with the best of them. For a while, the harlot of the highway lived with a Comanchero and then a Hell's Angel, but he was no angel, ending up with a two-year stint in the penitentiary for aggravated assault.

From then on, life became a litany of unfortunate incidents, which included many brushes with the law. Finally, Doris rescued the woman from her misery and introduced her to a more subdued family lifestyle. Could this woman have killed her sister's husband? Being an observer of countless quarrels between the two, it is not beyond the realms of possibility that little sister might have chosen to intervene. Daisy did help Hay Jude unload some of those bales, so the former bikie did have access to the pitchfork that penetrated her brother-in-law's torso in three places.

For the defence attorney, it proved a hard slog, as Marvin Green had never stood in a murder case, his speciality being conveyancing and family law—deals and divorce. In the interview room, his client became distant, detached, and disinterested. Not so her faithful companion, who crouched by the lawyer with bulging eyes and her tongue hanging out. Who would believe the legal eagle had Beef Jerky in his pocket?

Jude Ashbury's testimony helped the defence at a time when victories proved hard to come by. Yes, he tossed the pitchfork into his truck before he left the Shanahan property, but it must have fallen out of the vehicle on the bumpy piece of ground near the front gate. A fork in the road! The feed merchant did confirm that both sisters handled the tool, now classified as Exhibit A. Marvin Green let go with a gigantic sigh of relief. Those fingerprints would not be the damning evidence the prosecution thought they might be.

The beak in the highchair, your honour, Cash Silverman, had presided over many homicide cases, but, surely, he must have been surprised by such a rag-bag of jurors? The twelve men true included two women, a farmer, a boner from the abattoirs, and a barista from Starbucks. Silverman shouldn't have been officiating, being president of the golf club, with the victim a member, but the bar association declared no conflict of interest. Dan's bar bill must have been paid up.

The other contentious issue revolved around the presence of the Labrador in the courthouse. A prominent sign at the front of the building indicated animals were not allowed inside unless part of the proceedings, as in the case of the Crown v "Mad Dog" McGurk. The sadist, aka "Big Mac," chopped his victims into little pieces and barbecued them.

On the first day of the trial, the committed companion breezed past the exclusion notice, slipped by the guard at the courtroom entrance, and positioned herself beside her mistress and her legal team. The judge looked long and hard at the intruder, but he didn't do or say anything. On this occasion, Sophie behaved admirably, with only one lapse of concentration when the prosecutor raised his voice to make a point. The growl emanating from within not only scared the lawyer but pleased Justice Silverman. No need for any reprimand to come from him.

Nobody wanted to upset this arbitrator. In several controversial trials, he sent the accused to the gallows, thus acquiring the sobriquet "The Hanging Judge." The chap's wife, embarrassed by this tag, tried to soften his image.

"Cash is very good with wallpaper," she once told her neighbour.

Being a lion of litigation, Haydn Collingwood may have over-estimated his reputation and thought he possessed the status to impress and overawe these country yokels. No siree. The jury remained indifferent to his confident assertions and unmoved by his rhetoric. The boner from the abattoir had never heard so many big words before.

The appearance of Fred Farnsworth as a witness for the Crown didn't please anyone on the other side. Most people thought the guy would be arrested as the co-accused. Marvin Green hadn't anticipated the weasel making a deal, but realised an indemnity from prosecution is always a tantalising carrot to dangle in front of someone with a lot to lose. Although her opinion wasn't sought, Aunt Daisy came forth with her claim that the funeral director might be solely responsible for the dirty deed, the prize being an attractive woman and a landholding of some value.

"The slimy bugger! Would you be seen dead in his chapel?"

The professional mourner was disliked and distrusted around town, and many people reckoned all his plots weren't at the cemetery. Few people understood what Doris saw in him, although she maintained they were just friends.

"I was entitled to be in the reposing room. With Fred's mum ill, who else could prepare the flowers? You can't deny me a little earner on the side!"

Jude Asbury took to the stand to confirm his movements on the fatal Sunday and to try and explain the disappearance of an essential tool from his truck. Exhibit A, ever-present and erect beside the evidence stand, had been placed there by the prosecutor. Rather than lay the weapon of convenience across the table, he stood it on end, so the jurors might see the terrifying instrument of death in all its glory. Everybody had heard about Doris' fingerprints being found on the handle. The fact that Daisy's prints were also recovered from the same area indicated Counsellor Collingwood had been devious by neglecting to mention this fact, an omission that may not have gone down well with those who would soon be considering their verdict. What about the teeth marks, also on the handle of the pitchfork? This would become an item of curiosity further down the track.

Jude employed an apprentice, who he placed in charge of grain sales. Sandford Beach took some pride in this responsibility and looked forward to the day he would be promoted to assistant manager. Marv Green acted as his father's legal representative, and when Sandy approached the advocate with the hint that he might have valuable information, the barrister took him to lunch and grilled him on what he knew.

"You maintain that when you reported for work on Monday, there was a pitchfork in the back of the truck. Are you sure?"

"Yes, sir. We carry two such implements but one of them broke earlier in the week. Is this good news for your client?"

"Who knows," replied the confused lawyer. "It may be. Would you like some more coffee before we go back to the courthouse?"

Afternoons can be tedious in a courtroom if you're not pumped up on caffeine. Haydn Collingwood's declaration that the accused had motive, means, and murderous intent came across as provocative, as it should have been. After all, the Crown considered this crime to be a most diabolical act. The police possessed a body and a weapon, but the evidence was circumstantial. Did the jury realise this? Everyone looked forward to Mr Green's closing argument when they learned he would put Doris on the stand.

"Mrs Shanahan, when did you decide to kill your husband?"

Gasp, horror, shock, and pandemonium in the public gallery; even the stenographer appeared gobsmacked. Could this be right? This man was supposed to be leading the defence.

Cash Silverman called for silence and then let his gavel do the talking. With peace restored, those in attendance listened for her reply.

"I first thought about it around May but didn't do anything till July. Dan proved to be exceptionally obnoxious in July."

Hold the phone. Stop the press. Chaos in the court! Every journalist in attendance dashed for the door, with tomorrow's headlines uppermost in their thoughts. The cacophony of strident uproar proved louder than a Guns N' Roses concert, but above it all came the plaintiff howl of a dog in distress. Sophie didn't know what was going on, but she must have guessed the worst.

Of course, the media had gone off too early. Doris confessed to nothing illegal. Yes, she ordered a hard-to-detect poison, but parcel post in this country is unreliable, and the package didn't arrive until after Dan's demise. The smug defendant denied having anything to do with his death but congratulated the killer on an imaginative initiative.

In a black mark against transparency, she failed to mention that her lover kept a print of *American Gothic* on the wall of the reposing room at Farnsworth Funerals. This is the most famous painting in American art and features an elderly couple in front of their farm with a pitchfork.

One should remember Marvin Green represented Doris Shanahan and nobody else. However, the lady asked that they shouldn't try and implicate Freddie, who appeared to be playing for the other side, with a get-out-of-jail card as a reward. The funeral director's evidence hadn't hurt them. Would Haydn Collingwood hurt them? The accused eyed him off suspiciously, as he circled the witness box like a panther ready to pounce.

"You have told us, Mrs Shanahan, you had every intention of killing your husband. The opportunity arose, but you didn't take it. Somebody else killed him. Is that what you maintain?"

"I wasn't there when the opportunity arose. Otherwise, I might have killed him."

This comment brought a laugh from the gallery and a smile from the judge, although legal purists would be bound to regard such a remark as no laughing matter. With the jury warming to the accused, the prosecutor needed to regain his authority and assertiveness. The man was nobody's fool, although it looked as if he might be.

"What about Exhibit A, with your prints all over it? Right there in front of you, with dried blood on those three deadly prongs? Are you telling me you didn't thrust this gruesome tool through your man's alcohol-ravaged body and salivate as his life force drained from him?"

"My goodness, Mr Collingwood. You took the words right out of my mouth."

More laughter! Doris was as slippery as soap on a rope, and he didn't like it. Her confidence grew some with every question, and she appeared to be at ease with his verbal assault. The prosecution put forward accusations and assumptions, but no one could find a smoking gun.

Marvin Green recalled Jude Ashbury to the witness box and decided to tread warily. Sandy Beach may not have intended to put his boss in the frame, but if only one pitchfork returned to town with its owner, he might well be the murderer, not that the fellow had any motive anyone could see.

"When you arrived at the farm, prior to Pony Club, how many pitchforks did you take along?"

"We always carry two. No different that day. Both Mrs Shanahan and her sister mucked in and helped distribute the hay where it needed to be."

The interrogator paused before he continued his questioning. Two pitchforks made the case even more confusing.

"I have it on good authority that one of your tools was broken, and you went to Farm Hill with only one. Is this true?"

"Not true," said the local trader. "I replaced it on Saturday morning from Horace Hamilton's hardware store. That's the one by the table, there. One assumes it fell from the truck as I left the property."

So much for the Beach contribution. Now came the time to browbeat the expert from police forensics. Could this fellow be the weak link?

"Can you tell us about Exhibit A and whose fingerprints are on it?"

"Of course," replied a man who seemed to enjoy his few minutes in the public eye. He shared his answers with the lawyer and the jury, spicing them with a certain degree of theatrical chutzpah. The experienced expert sometimes turned to the judge and smiled. The judge smiled back.

"The tool is a standard three-pronged pitchfork, recently purchased, I suspect. The brand label is still in pristine condition, with only a few marks on the wooden grip. The fingerprints belong to Doris Shanahan, Daisy Doolittle and Dorothy Shanahan."

With young Dorothy's name revealed, there was a general intake of breath from those within earshot of the expert. Why hadn't this been mentioned before?

Why, indeed? Could this be an avenue of investigation that no one considered, least of all Doris, who understood the implications that might be drawn from this information? Judge Silverman had trouble controlling some outbursts from people who tried to trash Haydn Collingwood's credibility. Hadn't he heard of the truth, the whole truth, and nothing but the truth? The only person happy with this new revelation was Marvin Green, but his euphoria would be short-lived. The gentleman in the witness box straightened his bow tie and continued with his report.

"If you look carefully, you will see teeth marks on the handle of Exhibit A. Analysis has determined they belong to a three-year-old Labrador, with mild halitosis, tempered by a commercial mouthwash."

With this announcement, the judge, both lawyers, and most of the people in the room turned to stare at the contented canine, sitting by her mistress, aloof and impassive. Butter wouldn't melt in her mouth.

After Dan's body had been found, the boys in blue came around and fingerprinted the whole family except for Sophie, who did offer them her paw, but they just moved her on.

The adjournment had been a blessing. Now, with a minor involved, considerable thought would be given regarding her evidence. Dorothy, too young to be cross-examined, agreed to an interview with Marvin, who would include the girl's submission in his closing statement. In terms of the dog's evidence, nobody would get anything out of her. Sometimes, life can be a bitch.

Haydn Collingwood's summation proved to be eloquent but with little meat on the bones. Everyone looked bored as the grandstanding egotist prattled on for almost an hour. The prosecution lawyer eventually finished before the mid-day break, and his counterpart was invited to make his final presentation after lunch.

"Ladies and gentlemen of the jury, I want you to bear with me as I tell you a story, a story that will convince you Doris Shanahan did not kill her husband and leave you no option but to set her free with no stain on her reputation."

That last statement was a bit rich, considering the woman seemed prepared to poison her husband, and those shenanigans in the coffin room might just stain her reputation somewhat. Marvin had no experience with juries in a murder trial, but he did tell a super yarn. Just ask his children.

"When Daisy Doolittle accepted the invitation to live with her sister and her family, she felt obliged to contribute, and she did quite a lot. One of her achievements involved planting a petunia garden in the front of the house. Over time, she tutored Dorothy in the art of gardening and used her to collect mulch from the other side of the property. The wheelbarrow was in constant use and even instrumental in overcoming an embarrassing situation.

The garden patch below Dan's doghouse (this arrangement had been explained) was being doused by an insipid yellow liquid, which always appeared on the morning after Mr Shanahan had been carousing at the golf club. You guessed it. The poor fellow's wife would lock him out, and his deep sleep would be interrupted by the desire to relieve himself. The petunias must have been pissed-off."

This last comment was not appreciated by the judge, and he told the lawyer to limit his speculation to real-world observations and also advised the jury that they should disregard any opinions held by those in the garden bed. Marvin Green continued his final summation.

"As the person in charge of soil transition, Dorothy suggested they park the barrow over the petunia patch below the verandah on

Wednesdays and Sunday nights—the evenings when Dan managed to get plastered. The kid fancied herself as a problem solver."

Most of the jury started to tire of this tale, but the two women were entranced. Being avid gardeners, everything made sense to them. Why not use the empty cart to intercept the urine flow? Marvin continued.

"Now I come to the teeth marks on the supposed murder weapon. On that fateful Sunday, Dorothy, returning with her last mulch delivery, came upon Sophie with a tennis ball in her mouth. The dog had been playing fetch with David but, for some reason, returned the prize to the older sibling, who took it from her and hurled it as far as possible. The ball sailed over the front gate and landed on the road, with the playful pooch in hot pursuit.

The next time the girl saw the mutt, she was by the garden patch, and the animal arrived with a pitchfork in her mouth. Sophie is such an intelligent dog, she must have realised this was lost property and wanted to return the tool, probably expecting a treat as a reward."

Members of the jury stiffened appreciably, as did those in the public gallery. Marvin noticed this. Doris also. Even the dog observed people looking at her. Now for the *coup de grâce*; the father of four crossed his fingers and finished his tale.

"What did Dorothy do? I'll tell you what she did. She accepted the pitchfork offered to her, and placed it upright in the crutch of the wheelbarrow, between one of the shafts and the steel tray, with little thought that this could be dangerous and the wrong thing to do. Let's not blame the girl.

On this particular Sunday, Dan got smashed at the golf club. A mate, having scored a hole-in-one, shouted the bar, as you do, and his friend over-imbibed. The used car dealer arrived home to a locked door and settled down on his stretcher, where he passed out. This is conjecture, but witnesses have rated his drinking on this day as "over and above anything they had seen before." Imagine all that amber fluid, just waiting to get out.

What state do you think he was in when he staggered to the edge of the porch? As full as the last bus, I would think.

And it had been raining, making the deck slippery. Maybe he put his hand on the rail but didn't see the chewed-up remains of David's Star Wars robot under his feet. Half-asleep, he stood on it, lost his balance, crashed through the railing, and fell on the upright prongs of the pitchfork. His weight would have been too much for the handle to bear, so he tumbled into the barrow, which then rolled down the hill to the front gate. This is where the milkman found him later in the morning."

Marvin's final remarks were delivered with candour and theatrical finesse, culminating in a sincere request for the jury to abide by their remit—a decision beyond a reasonable doubt. The silence in the courtroom exemplified his achievement. Cue the proverbial pin drop. The only person who wanted to say something was Haydn Collingwood, but the judge waved him away before clearing his throat and addressing the jury. He waxed lyrical about legalities and then sent them out to consider their verdict. What more could he do? Cash Silverman seemed as bewildered as everyone else.

The not guilty judgement made headlines across the country, and Marvin Green emerged as an instant celebrity. Over the ensuing months, Labrador sales reached a peak never experienced before, and Daisy Doolittle became a spokesperson for flower power.

Doris and Freddie enjoyed their quiet celebration in the coffin room, a bottle of Champagne under the *American Gothic* painting. Sophie just lay on her back as her mistress rubbed her tummy. How good was that?

THE DANCING DOGS
OF DONNYBROOK

Coming from Donnybrook, you would expect the breed to be boxers, but not so, although I concede that there were a few street fighters in the district, mostly owned by members of the IRA. My father was a member of this particular organisation, and I can remember channelling much of his invective into a part of my brain which I called "The Blarney Bucket."

The dogs were Beagles: Paul, George, John, and Ringo. Billy Fitzpatrick didn't even own a leg, but he did control the mangy misfits. They followed him everywhere, and that meant Mrs O'Shaughnessy's Irish dancing class every Saturday morning in her hired space. The lad may not have wanted to be there, but at fourteen years of age, it is difficult to assert one's opinion in a world dominated by adults.

I suspect his four-legged friends were rather bemused by it all, but dogs are outstanding mimics, and it wasn't long before the hard-kicking hounds trod the boards with purpose and panache. Even the teacher seemed impressed.

The quirky quartet didn't tour until after their appearance on late-night television. In Ireland, a late night is around 9 p.m., and the RTE studio was situated just down the road. This allowed young Billy to appear with the host and wax lyrical about the clever canines. Most people were aware of Beagles because they were confronted by them every time they tried to sneak their cannabis past the customs people. In America, Charlie Brown's pal Snoopy won the hearts and minds of kids from Kansas to Kalamazoo, but who believed the little guys could dance?

"We all dance to a yellow Tamborine," their debut performance on television, rated well, and viewers would have to go back a couple of years to remember anything so riveting. However, The Yodelling

Chickens never consolidated their appeal and ended up in a microwave. The step-dancing quartet ended up in America on tour. This suited Ringo because he came from Cancún, and was gagging for an enchilada or two, always available in the land of the free.

I know you're going to ask, "How does a mongrel from Mexico end up in Dublin?"

It's a long story, but it's your money.

In the basement of the British Embassy in Washington, a secretive group go about their business with stealth and furtive enthusiasm. Charles, Nigel, Amanda and the dog called LeBron were all members of MI6 and committed to protecting UK interests in that part of the world. These were not their real names. Amanda and LeBron (real name Winston) drew the short straw and flew to Cancún to investigate a drug problem emanating out of that city.

Aware of the cocaine pouring into a certain gangster-run nightclub in the East End of London, the intelligence agency traced the source back to this holiday resort in Mexico. Their lead agent attempted to liaise with the local immigration people, which wasn't easy because most were at the beach.

"Excuse me, senor. We are at the point of departure at this fine airport but I see no dogs."

"Ahhh, senorita, you have come to the wrong place. The dog, he is at the incoming hall."

Amanda and her British Bulldog looked at each other. Could they be thinking the same thing?

What kind of idiot would smuggle drugs into Mexico? What customs department would only have one sniffer dog?

They met the Beagle called Ringo and, with permission, escorted him over to the departure lounge. Border Control had isolated one suspect, a vision-impaired man who made many return journeys to England but not to London. His destination was Liverpool. A blind man's companion is often a Labrador or Golden Retriever. This chap travelled with a St. Bernard, and his declaration sounded doubtful.

"For what reason are you coming to Mexico?"

"I'm here for the skiing."

"Senor, there is no snow in Cancún."

"I was misinformed."

It took the respective agencies some months to realise the liquid cocaine was in the barrel around the dog's neck. On one trip, the blind man fell asleep, and the passenger next to the animal chose to un-tap some of the brandy expected to be in the barrel. The cabin crew found him dead on arrival.

In Liverpool, the customs people relied on panting Paul, but he proved to be hopeless. His nose was only interested in females, and he must have let so many drug bunnies through the net. The incoming flight from Mexico would be his last job for king and country before a meeting with another disappointment in the disgraced dog's compound.

Due to difficulties with LeBron's paperwork, Amanda boarded the plane with Ringo riding shotgun, sitting one back across the aisle from the courier and not far from the kitchen. In hindsight, perhaps the crew did get a little too friendly with the Beagle. After all, he was adorable. They certainly shouldn't have given him access to the galley, but he did look hungry.

With the focus off the drug runner, he slipped the security net while the first-class passengers screamed blue murder because the dog ate their dinner. Ringo would never see Cancún again. Placed in an auction job lot with Paul, he and his new best friend would be transported across the water to await a fate worse than death—Irish stew and soda bread.

The other two dancing dogs would not be sold into slavery. John was found wandering alone in the main street of Johnstown, Kilkenny, and George, an out-of-work actor, felt unloved since his last commercial for bacon. The four of them met in a lost dog's home in Dublin, and Billy Fitzpatrick received three euros a day to take them for walkies.

Now the superstars shined bright in America, with the world their oyster.

Can you imagine how many people put their hands up when the promoters went looking for a chaperone? Billy was too young, so Shauna O'Shaughnessy won the job. A wise choice! This lady, stern but fair, wouldn't let any of these smooth-talking entrepreneurs take her down. One also needed to maintain those dance routines. Once you become a professional, even the slightest fault will be noticed.

The first whistle-stop was New York, and Amanda and LeBron drove up from Washington to see the performance at the Radio City Music Hall, the Showplace of the Nation. The full-house sign went up and the Beagles didn't disappoint. The double act with the Rockettes was a showstopper. The mayor enjoyed the entertainment so much that he invited the fearless four to display their talent at the Bronx Zoo. This show didn't go so smoothly. The monkeys wouldn't stop chattering, the giraffes couldn't see a thing, and the sole hyena laughed at all the wrong moments. That's show business for you.

With more Irish people in New York than in Dublin, that segment entitled "St. Paddy's Quickstep" won over the harshest critic. For Chicago, they changed it to "Hold the phone, Capone" and found themselves some Italian fans. This was the high point of the tour. Las Vegas was much anticipated, but the punters had other things on their minds. The tapping didn't resonate with everyone, even if heard above the noise of the slot machines. By the time the group reached Santiago, fatigue had set in, and morale wasn't good. Cast and crew looked forward to returning home, including the dog from around these parts.

Santiago is a whistle and a whiff away from the Mexican border, and that tantalising treat that is a tasty Tijuana taco. In between the end of the entertainment and the wrap party, Ringo disappeared into the night, never to be seen again, although, months later, somebody reported hearing about a dog performing a one-man cabaret at a nightclub in Puerto Vallarta.

Back in Dublin, Billy Fitzpatrick now only walked three buddies, so they docked his pay by 25%. Mrs O'Shaughnessy increased the size of her studio by the same margin, due to the popularity of her famous students, with a rumour that the pope was keen to learn step-dancing. It was a pity no one showed much interest in what the dogs wanted because Ringo wasn't alone as far as home-sickness was concerned; Paul missed his pals from the pound at UK Revenue and Customs in Merseyside. Everyone in this facility understood he had the hots for Eleanor, and his mate Rigby was terrific company. Having seen Billy's dad achieve positive results from his wife by whining, the magnificent mimic implemented a similar strategy with the head of housing at his new digs—same area but a little more upmarket, as befits a demidog of the dance.

"This mutt won't shut up, Shauna, and he won't stay in the naughty corner. Where is the self-discipline you taught him?"

Mrs O had never been lucky in love, but she understood that the little fella was as randy as a robber's dog. She didn't know about Eleanor and would never condone a loose arrangement with any of the riff-raff that patrolled the streets of South Dublin. George and John were happy enough, back in the environment they were used to, although George had taken to urinating by the statue of Oscar Wilde in Merrion Park, possibly not the only one.

The tour to the United States had been well-reported in Britain, and there was some embarrassment in northern parts that they had mistreated their guy so badly; exporting him to the Emerald Isle. Not everyone has a nose for drugs. The editor of the Liverpool Echo had a nose for a story, but he didn't want to send his best reporter across the Irish Sea. There were alternatives in the newsroom.

"Jimmy, I want a human interest angle on this dog in Dublin: his background in law enforcement, girlfriends, possible criminal contacts, etc. You understand what our readers want—how we loved him and yet cut him loose. Get me tears dripping on the page."

"Gee, boss," said the young journalist. "I don't speak dog. What about Lois, the new girl who owns a cocker spaniel? Or Penny Lane, her sister! She would be good."

She would be good, thought the editor, *if I didn't have so many personnel holes to plug. Bloody staff shortages!* Those winter chills were rampant, but so far, the lass with the economics degree looked hale and hearty.

"Penny reports for our financial section. I suppose I could send her with you to check out your expense account."

Jimmy caught the next plane to the Irish capital and was back within twenty-four hours without a dent in his expense account. He recorded interviews with Mrs O'Shaughnessy, Billy Fitzpatrick, and the Archbishop of Dublin, who all maintained that Liverpool's loss was Ireland's gain. None of them wanted to explain the dog's current grumpy disposition because they couldn't. Nobody realised the petulant pooch was pining for his princess.

Jimmy's poignant piece, which appeared on a slow news day, changed everything. Just like one of those prisoner swaps during the Cold War, Paul was repatriated to his former place of abode, and Trinity College received back Miles Grunt, the prickly poet of punk, who walked on the wild side of woke.

"Glad to have you back, Miles," said Daphne Doolan, the ever-suffering provost of this elite academy of learning.

"Get knotted," replied the notorious one, as surly as ever and not happy to be frogmarched out of England.

Life is not easy when you are cut off from your friends, is it? George and John must have been depressed, if not despondent, now that the boogie brothers were down to two. A certain promoter rushed around trying to fast-track replacements, but you don't grow twinkle-toes overnight.

In the meantime, the two stay-at-home Beagles found themselves with not much to do. With hope more than confidence, George's manager relisted him with his casting agency, and can you believe what happened next? The Ford Motor Company hired him to front a series of advertisements, which they called "Dancing with the Cars."

Television can do wonders for your image. On tour, George was marginalised by being one of a group, and their act didn't transmit into millions of homes across the country like these vehicle commercials, supported by print and outdoor advertising throughout Europe and the USA. Some folks thought the Beagle had replaced the eagle as America's pre-eminent symbol of freedom; especially with the dog of the moment cruising along the coast in a classic Ford Mustang. No, he wasn't driving.

The photo shoots with Kim Kardashian in New York were a bonus, as not many buxom beauties frequented the O'Shaughnessy classes (something to do with equilibrium). Such a sweetie, and she always produced treats on the set. How good was that?

The kidnapping was a dark day in the history of advertising, and being a former member of this profession, I am reluctant to give it much oxygen.

The finger of suspicion pointed towards the "black bag" unit at Chevrolet, who were haemorrhaging and hadn't hit a home run since the hound came on the scene. A lot of people wanted to know how the abduction happened and questioned security arrangements.

"The mutt was there one minute, and then he was gone. I don't understand," moaned the beleaguered minder.

"Yeah, yeah, yeah," said the photographer. "We saw that security guard. He only had eyes for Ms Kardashian, and he was drooling."

The police were thorough and concerned for George's safety and well-being.

"Is the victim a diabetic? Does he need insulin or anything like that?" said the investigating officer, who thought this crime should have been shunted off to the dog squad. With the media pack coming at him, he re-evaluated and realised the ramifications of any story involving a famous personality.

The next morning, the headlines said it all—"Downtown Dognap." George was now the hottest dog since Chili Gidget, the Taco Bell Chihuahua. Ford offered a reward, and KK was in tears.

"What's happened to my best pal?" she cried. The Pomeranians luxuriating in her mansion pretended not to hear that comment. A celebrity with so many endorsement responsibilities deserves the benefit of the doubt.

The go-to detective for such kidnaps was Duke Devine. These kinds of crimes against birds and beasts were not uncommon, and he issued instructions to round up the usual suspects. With a vibrant market for quality pets, certain individuals worked off a shopping list. On the other hand, if someone phoned through a ransom demand, the prospective outcome might be far more alarming. Devine's partner, recently transferred from Traffic, had ideas.

"What about jealousy among the other TV stars? This kind of thing happens all the time. The new kid on the block arrives on the scene and takes all the glory."

If Duke thought this a reasonable assumption, he didn't say so.

"Did you have anyone in mind?"

"Well, those meerkats are everywhere, and that Energizer Bunny might be slowing down."

"Enough, I get the picture."

In reality, this was not a picture that painted a thousand words, and Duke Devine remained the smartest detective in the room.

When George awakened from his deep sleep, he found his movement restricted. The dog was in a cage.

It was not a comfortable confinement and not the only cage in the room. Across the way, a gigantic Mastiff lay on his belly, looking alert but bored. The orange-bellied parrot was making all the noise. The bird had also been kidnapped, living quarters and all, but nobody likes to be deposited downwind from a striped polecat, one of the smelliest creatures around.

How would George cope with all this? One moment he was cavorting with a Kardashian, and now he was in lock-up with some of the rarest species on Earth. Would he be fed? What about physical exercise? The consummate professional always liked to keep in shape.

The parrot finally gave it a rest, and one could hear part of the discussion coming from the next room, a telephone conversation. It wasn't hard to recognise the nationality of the speaker this end. The kidnapper was Irish.

"To be sure, I've got the dancing dog, and if you've got the cash, I'm ready to exchange. Would you be happy for this afternoon, now?"

The exchange took place on a bench in Central Park, and the dog was transferred from a cage to a leash and able to walk to his waiting conveyance, a Bentley Mulsanne, renowned for its comfort, quality, and style.

The owner of the luxury car, Martha Mandeville, was the widow of industrialist Mitchell Mandeville and a resident of Long Island. With George perched beside the chauffeur in the front seat, this was where they were heading. She would be waiting for the canine with a bowl filled to the brim with Nutra Complete, the most expensive dog food on the planet, with forty ingredients in every bite. The woman would let him settle in before asking him to perform his hops and bops.

Martha was not a bad person. The chauffeur was the bad person. If he knew she wanted something that money couldn't buy, he would utilise his friends on the dark side to procure same. Turning a blind eye, as she did, didn't exclude her from complicity, and such a situation must have gnawed at her conscience. Only a serious religious person would convert one of the rooms in their mansion to a chapel so that she could be close to God.

Some people are probably wondering what motivated the dame to even want a dancing dog. The answer is glorified by history. Martha had been a budding artiste when she met her husband, and although he didn't advertise this fact among his neighbours on Long Island, he became the handbag on her arm at many theatrical productions. Together, they saw and salivated over Fred Astaire, Isadora Duncan, Ginger Rogers, and Cyd Charisse. Mitchell was well gone when his wife attended her last production at the Radio City Music Hall. George, with his magnificent moves, totally captivated her. She just had to have him.

On arrival, the Beagle appeared to be a little lost, the house being so huge, but he followed his nose and discovered the food with forty ingredients in every bite. The petting was put on hold until he completed his dinner, but then Martha moved in, and the new resident didn't resist. The gal had a light touch and didn't smell too bad. If only he knew how much that perfume cost.

The next few days were days of discovery, with George getting the run of the house, although they did lock all the doors in case the little guy bolted. With each meal, he became more compliant and accustomed to his surroundings, which became more expansive when they let him outside, to the chagrin of the gardener. Beagles do like to dig, particularly when trying to find a place for future bone deposits.

On most nights, George would produce his best routines for his new mistress, and she would take him through her scrapbook. He must have been impressed that she once played The Palace and also the Bijou and Roxy theatres. Martha couldn't wait to unleash her recently acquired friend on her old friends, with a full-on cocktail party. Details of this plan were passed to the chauffeur via the housekeeper.

"Oh no," cried the shifty one. "As soon as they learn this fella is the kidnapped canine, I'm going to be breaking rocks at Rikers."

How would the Bentley driver explain to his employer that a party wouldn't be a smart idea? She didn't need to know all the specifics but would have to understand her role as an accessory after the fact. The lady of the house was aghast when confronted with this news, and remorseful, so much so that a visit to the chapel was required. This is where George found her—rosary beads in hand and an anguished look on her face. He snuggled in beside his new mentor and squatted on the pew with his tongue hanging out. Let's face it. Sometimes humans can forget dinner time.

There are some obscure angelic figures in the Catholic Church, and one of these is St. Denise of the Dance, Martha's preferred pious person when things aren't working out as they should. Apparently, Denise learnt her moves from Salome but was too modest to dispense with all seven veils.

On the back of multiple novenas, Martha decided that her driver was too nice a chap to go to prison and cancelled the get-together. She dedicated the rest of her life to the well-being of her pet and wrote him into her will, unaware that you can kill with kindness. The woman over-fed the greedy bugger until he lost his ability to perform and ended up obese with dog bloat. The poor creature failed to respond to any kind of diet and died three days before his mistress. Some weeks later, the chauffeur travelled to Manhattan in the dead of night and left his casket outside the stage door of the Radio City Music Hall.

Then there was one.

Perhaps John missed his compatriots, but if so, it wasn't obvious. Billy Fitzpatrick, now seventeen and his full-time carer, helped him spend his acquired fortune, with membership at the Milltown Golf Club, not to mention the holiday house on the Algarve and a charge account at Petbarn. The dog didn't need to confirm these contracts, as everyone trusted Billy's acumen and excellent business sense. He was a Borstal Boy with lots of street cred and great expectations.

In between golf games, the teenager did look after the little nipper quite well, always ready for a walk in the park. I'm not sure whether John enjoyed the Hurling at Croke Park, but he was keen on their sojourns to Phoenix Park, where Miles Grunt, enfant terrible of the literary world, often read poetry from a soapbox. Dog walkers could be enticed over to the readings by the poet's followers, who handed out jerky to the passers-by.

On one occasion, Miles invited the toe-tapper onto the soapbox, and the demonstrative dancer produced one of his most exciting routines, with Billy signing autographs on his behalf. Because of his abrasive nature, Grunt possessed few friends, but he seemed to connect with the easy-going lad and his talented side-kick, so they retired to the nearest pub to reflect on relevant issues and the world order. The patrons recognised the two celebrities in the bar, so the visitors didn't have to put their hands in their pockets, and a lot of the Guinness overflow ended up in the dog bowl.

When you don't have to pay for your drinks, leaving can be such sweet sorrow. However, departure seemed prudent. Both Miles and Billy struggled to stagger in a straight line, and the dog was walking backwards for Christmas (that's the title of a song). In the aftermath of this reckless revelry, the young man sought remedial salvation at the pharmacy, and the fragile sniffer may have decided to embrace abstinence. Certainly, he would try to avoid any further contact with the pickled poet.

Folks in the area around Donnybrook had a lot of time for the brilliant Beagle. The local hero enjoyed the trappings of wealth and prestige, but he also did many fine things for the community, having won Municipal Dog of the Month several times. He even became involved with the Secret Service, just like his pal Ringo did.

At the time, China was seen as an imminent threat to world peace, and the entreaties of Miss Universe contestants did nothing to alleviate the threat. The Secret Service had uncovered the presence of a Chinese cabal in Ireland, which received their briefings from someone from the Beijing to Broadway Theatre Company in the West End of London. Their current production was *101 Dalmatians, The Musical.*

In an extravagant effort to promote the musical outside of England, some PR smartie sent twenty-six Dalmatians (one for each county in the republic) to Dublin, a horror situation for quarantine staff. MI6 discovered that critical information had been microchipped onto one of the dogs, destined to find itself in the hands of the top Chinese spy in that country, Paddy Chang.

Did the operatives need to be so clandestine? "What's wrong with the Royal Mail?"

They say you shouldn't ask a question unless you know the answer, so perhaps this was a valid consideration.

One of the travelling group found himself with one extra black spot on his person, and authorities needed to flush out the messenger without endangering international sensitivities. The usual sniffers might be overexcited and offensive, so they reached out to the step dancer with acknowledged theatrical experience. Johnny came to the immigration hall, searching for a microchip. When he confronted the dog with the digital implant, the little guy performed a short adagio routine in front of the pooch, indicating that the unwitting mule would be burdened with another add-on: a tracking device.

Billy and the Beagle were invited to the showdown, which turned out to be in Wicklow Town. That's where the wired Dalmatian led them. Five members of the Garda and two MI6 operatives sealed the deal. Paddy Chang didn't have a chance.

Shanghai Travel, his company, slipped under the guard of the intelligence agencies. Wicklow is a picturesque part of Ireland, but Chang's hot air spy balloons didn't bother with that, hovering over military installations, restricted locations, and even the Guinness Brewery. Can you blame them for that?

Irish Republicans don't like to receive chest candy from the Brits, but the Dublin dynamo was proud of his medal, which arrived with a personal letter from James Bond. Young Mr Fitzpatrick let everyone read this communication for a small fee. International relations, being what they are, precluded any public trial, and the Beagle didn't get the acclaim he deserved. Having said that, some folks thought he ought to stop sticking his nose in other people's business.

This should have been the end of it, but what's a party without punch? The coverts caught Chang but not his network. His trusted deputy resided in Dublin, and it proved difficult for the good guys to track her down because she wasn't Chinese. Belinda had messy morning hair, and her cheeks were as puffy as a blowfish at a barbecue. As a large woman, the super-sized spy was more comfortable in loose-fitting clothing and trundled along the street like a ragman's runabout. You couldn't imagine a less-likely espionage agent.

Nevertheless, she spoke Mandarin like a native and could stab you with chopsticks or drown you in green tea. Few people were aware that Belinda's father had been a communist agitator in Nanjing before returning to Dublin to become a game show host. With her confrere now in jail, responsibility now lay with this daughter of darkness, and revenge was very much on the table.

"Tell me, Liam O bloody Rourke. Do you kill dogs, or are you only interested in pigs and British maggots?"

"Well, now, if that's not an interesting proposal. What would you be payin' me to dispose of the poor thing? I would have to waive me personal feelings, given we are talkin' about man's best friend."

Would it surprise anyone that O'Rourke boasted friends in the animal kingdom? Most of them were weasels. It would only be a matter of time before he departed the public house, happy with the price on John's head. This is not a conclusion that I would have hoped for when I started writing this story, with only one hero remaining to talk about, and he is about to end up as Chop Suey Chow Mein.

Of course, it's not over till it's over, is it? The potential victim was saved by the bells. Not so Mr O'Rourke, who stepped out of the pub and attempted to cross the road as a red fire truck came screeching around the corner with all bells ringing. The urgency of this arrival impressed everyone except the chap standing in the path of the utility vehicle.

The Garda arrested Belinda at the graveyard. Being the only person to turn up at Liam's funeral, apart from his dog, the wallopers ransacked her apartment as a matter of course and discovered damning material that linked her to Paddy Chang and fellow operatives Declan Hong and Cormac Kong.

Although the brave Beagle didn't need to resort to violence to round up the remaining members of this insipid triad, the government still awarded him a canine MBE (Most Barks Ever). The Variety Club also confirmed him as a life member.

I suspect they don't have a Register of Heroes in Dublin, but they should. The Donnybrook dancer would not be out of place beside Michael Collins, James Joyce, Val Doonican and Bono. It's your call, Prime Minister.

Note: This story, a remnant from my father's "Blarney Bucket," is intended to venerate Irish dancing and the man who made it an international phenomenon, Michael Flatley. I believe he and Mrs O'Shaughnessy broke bread in New York.

MIND YOUR PEAS
AND QUEUES

Richard, a struggling actor, had no money. The fellow hadn't wanted to leave his digs, but city life was expensive, and he had burned a few bridges. Stratford, a small settlement in the Southern Highlands, appealed to residents and tourists alike. Many people came to this hamlet (the place didn't have a church) to communicate with nature. It was a town without ambition until Richard arrived. Twelve months later, they came to visit the "Big Pea Pod." One can only guess why. The "Big Banana" and the "Big Pineapple" were successful tourism destinations in northern parts, and Richard saw potential in Vegetable Valley.

He came up with the idea of injecting Viagra into the pea crops, with the result for all to see. The new arrival also started a Shakespearean theatre company, and promoted the annual frog-jumping championships, a great day out. On one of these occasions he met his future bride but more about that later.

The drama group consisted of six people, and they needed to fight for priority at the civic hall, the only building of its type in what was predominantly an English village in an Australian setting. Early in the week, the Boy Scouts, Girl Guides, and Country Women's Association dominated the meeting space, and on Saturday night, the local movie mogul prevailed. Richard acquired Sunday rights after negotiations with the debating club, the Stratford Choir, and Harriet's Highland Dancers.

Off-stage, the actor did not project an imposing presence, being rather small, a little overweight and short-sighted. The fellow did possess his own hair, although there were signs of follicles wanting to jump ship. Once engrossed in his various roles, a different story emerged. The depth of his emotional orations proved awe-inspiring, and those who came to criticise and condemn would be left with nowhere to go—the taming of the few.

The man played Coriolanus in Sydney opposite Vivien Bee, proving him to be no second banana. The media tried to concoct a romance between the two, but it was much ado about nothing. Vivien, being older than her leading man, would have harboured reservations about his reputation as a lecherous Lothario. Yes, there had been a marriage duly dissolved before he decamped to Stratford, the future home of the frog-jumping championships.

♣

The virgin, Prudence Godbolt, born and bred in the Southern Highlands, survived her education with the nuns at the Benedictine convent in Melbourne. On returning to her hometown, she was well equipped to ward off the advances of the salacious types who presented their credentials in a most ungentlemanly way. Over time, Pru accepted her single existence and enjoyed the companionship provided by her two terriers, Mac and Beth.

Mac/Beth

Need I mention that the lady sat in the audience for all of the performances of the Shakespearean Theatre Group? She couldn't wait to greet the star of the show, and this happened at the Miss Piggy Lunch during the frog-jumping championships. Little Richard, at that time squiring a woman called Lucille, was delighted to be introduced to the schoolteacher. After all, older people don't meet a virgin very often.

Several widows and divorcees lived in the town, and the chap's diminutive presence didn't deter them one bit. Neither did it deter Prudence, who charmed the pants off him. Captivated by her dark eyes, distinctive diction, and dignified disposition, he only needed to pass scrutiny from the dogs to win her heart and mind. This wouldn't be easy. Richard had no experience with animals, although he won a small part in the movie *Babe*, which involved a pig as the leading player.

"Beth likes you, but I'm not sure about Mac. Why don't you take him for walkies? The two of you can bond without any girls to cramp your style."

It didn't surprise the actor to find Beth in his corner, as he always felt more at ease with females. Walkies would be a whole new ball game, as he had no knowledge of the conventions relating to fetch and dog-walking, particularly the requirement to pick up their mess.

"You've got to be kidding. I have to collect and dispose of the shit?"

There would be a lot of tense moments in their marriage, but in the aftermath of the honeymoon, the groom was ready to be manipulated. Those dog walks would be the first test of his commitment. Each morning, they would stretch out with the dogs and take turns being the crap collector. However, the male escort continued to forget his responsibility, only to be reminded by his ever-alert wife.

"Richard—the turd!"

Nobody would tell Richie that he might end up as a hen-pecked husband, but the signs looked ominous. Pru indicated she was keen to make up for lost time, with babies on the agenda. Her brother Edward, the third member of her family to produce children, always made himself available to dish out advice. The font of all wisdom claimed that if you lived with dogs, you should be able to cope with kids. His counsel to Richard was more definitive.

"Get on top of this dog thing, or it might be love's labour lost." Eddie understood how to talk to a Shakespearian actor.

Those who opt for a tree change don't always go all the way and become farmers, but Stratford possessed the right conditions for growing peas. However, I'm not sure the peas were ready for Richard and his Viagra. Yes, he toiled in the soil and built a trellis for the climbers, but they had to listen to his monologues all day, especially on those weeks preceding the opening of a new show.

A typical run would be two weeks, but by the twelfth night, there would hardly be anyone in the audience. Pru stacked the seats with her pals from the CWA, and they always discussed the performance at book club. God help those who criticised her husband. The professional critic, employed by the *Southern Highlands News*, lived in Bowral. The guy always received a presentation pack of peas before making his journey into the backblocks.

Henry Tudor appeared as the spring growth turned the town into a target for tourists. He purchased the local flower shop and joined the Shakespearean Theatre Group as member number seven. The good-looking dude in his early thirties arrived with excellent review clippings, deeming him a capable actor. The group now boasted a young leading man, and Richard was not pleased. The upstart from Richmond also presented the leading lady with a garland of roses; all Richie offered were peas. It's enough to make you want to go home and beat up your wife.

This didn't happen, but it could have. The man experienced a difficult three months as winter provided little rain, and his pea yield looked dry and parched. If it wasn't for the dogs peeing on the crop, who knows where he might be? Such a challenging time for everybody! The usually busy camping supply store did a "Winter of our Discount Tents" promotion, but they still came up short.

During rehearsals at the civic hall, Richard didn't make Henry welcome. The senior man came across as grumpy and competitive, and it took one of the lesser lights to explain how they might be able to make things work. At the time, *The Island of Dr Moreau* was booked as Saturday's movie offering. Michael York portrayed the young man and Burt Lancaster the older Dr Moreau. The two thespians related to York and Lancaster, as they had both played Richard III and Henry VII, so they buried the hatchet the following day (just as Henry had done on Bosworth Field).

At home, the new husband learnt to live with the dogs, and they appreciated his fraternisation efforts. Every week, the terriers were taken to McDonald's, and Richard even gave them a part in his production of *Romeo and Juliet*, with Henry playing the lead. The energy of the star-crossed lovers must have rubbed off on the canines because Mac started humping Beth halfway through the second act, much to the delight of the audience. This would be the end of their stage careers.

For the young women of the town, the arrival of an unmarried stud in the form of Henry proved to be a godsend. The girls flocked to his flower shop, and the bold ones announced their intentions. Were they the customers responsible for his thriving business? Other shopkeepers looked on in envy, but Richard embraced the motivation of another to open his own retail outlet.

The Pantry offered everything pea, and items such as pea soup and peanuts were products that had to be possessed. This venture proved to be profitable, but so many others didn't get off the ground. One evening, he experienced a midsummer night's dream which turned into a nightmare. Should he utilise the pond on his property to help breed Peking ducks, which he would sell to Chinese restaurants throughout the Highlands? Yes, he should. Prudence thought the quackers would be a soft option for her newborn children, as the terriers were a little rough around the edges. Of course, nothing ever goes as planned. Pru failed to get pregnant, and the dogs and ducks hated each other. As a peace negotiator, the duck breeder disappointed, and the water birds ended up on the table at Christmas.

The yuletide season in Australia can be quite hot, and outdoor activities are the norm. A town like Stratford is a magnet for holidaymakers in their caravans and motor homes. Since his arrival, Richard had made his mark with his promotions, including the January contribution *Dog Day Afternoon*. The festivities started with the Al Pacino movie on Saturday night, followed by canine events the next day. Consider a Best in Show competition, Poodle Pranks, Working for the Man, and the Kibble King, sponsored by a leading pet food manufacturer. Some folks called it hell on a Sunday.

The big winner on the day was always the owner of the hardware store. Because he possessed a license to sell rifles, the locals referred to him as "The Merchant of Menace," but on this occasion, he sold more gumboots than he did for the rest of the year. With so much dog crap on the oval, everybody should be prepared. Neither Mac nor Beth won a thing, but this didn't worry Richard, who claimed all the registration fees. His only outlay would be a donation to the football club plus the cost of grass purification.

Another innovation saw an outdoor production of *As You Like It*. Nobody liked it, but you pay your money and hope for the best. Cross-dressing might be acceptable in the city, but country folks weren't having a bar of it. They also booed when "Orlando" didn't turn out to be Orlando Bloom.

"Don't beat yourself up, sweetheart," said Prudence. "The concept was fine. You managed a full house, but they expected a Bloom and got a Stratford florist."

Notwithstanding the negative reviews for this complicated comedy, the female lead was in demand. Over at the "Big Pea Pod," she doubled as Miss Sweetpea, the Green Queen. The body painting, a labour of love for local artist Milton Blotch, helped the illusion. The chap specialised in beautiful birds. In this instance, he forgot to make allowances for the weather. Once the temperature reached thirty degrees centigrade, the paint started to run, and the young lady ended up looking like a mushy version of the vegetable. At times like this, a cup of iced pea is more than acceptable.

One can go on about life in a country town in Australia, but let's face it—I'm not paid by the Tourism Commission. The communities in these towns are quite pragmatic. Was it King Lear who said, "Love me or leave me?" Perhaps it was Doris Day.

As I conclude this tale of passion and opportunity, I can assure you that Shakespeare is alive and well in Stratford, with Richard watching his peas and queues. Should the queues continue to lengthen, he will grow old knowing that all's well that ends well.

Note: Fifteen of the bard's most popular plays are buried in this trite tribute. Uncover them if you must. In the meantime, think kindly of Mac and Beth. They remain blacklisted.

A PREGNANT PAUSE

Now, I want you to hear this.

THE TART FROM HOLLAND PARK

The nuns held high hopes for Natasha when she left the convent. They maintained a vested interest in the girl, who arrived on their doorstep as a refugee from Ukraine, but the decision to sponsor her through an economics degree was courageous, to say the least. In her first semester with them, and since then, the new arrival struggled with her sums. In the end, it didn't matter. She became a prostitute.

When you are on the game, it is important to try and acquire a point of difference to separate you from the also-rans. So, Tash advertised herself as Madame Lash, and rented a small dungeon in the basement of a three-story terrace in Holland Park; a discreet address in a respectable part of town.

The other tenants couldn't help but notice the stream of men who visited the princess of pain at all hours of the day and night, but they turned a blind eye. However, the screams and other blood-curdling noises emanating from down below couldn't be moderated. The neighbours refused to turn a deaf ear and reported the mistress of misery to the rozzers at the local precinct, unaware that the chief constable was a regular customer.

The lady emerged from the experience with a slap on the wrist, but her client base developed a nervous complaint, and business dried up, forcing her to look for a real job. She went to McDonald's, citing her financial expertise. They gave her work peeling onions.

One should remember that most of Macca's workforce is barely pubescent, and they rarely employ convent girls. Those chicks go to Domino's or Pizza Hut. So, don't cry for Natasha. After the onions, she might graduate to front of house and possibly end up as the big cheese. For the moment, she earned enough money to pay the rent, but life can be lonely without the excitement of a grown man grovelling at your feet with a dog chain around his neck. Hey, that's the answer. Get a dog.

Zelda, the Whippet, stood out at Bow Wow London, displaying poise, personality, and a loving lick. What more could you want? The manager guaranteed she would poo in private and respect members of the opposite sex. After all, madam had every intention of returning to her former lifestyle when the heat died down.

It would have been easier if the animal had arrived with a book of instructions. The young woman, never having owned a pet before, was ill-prepared for the twenty-four-hour commitment.

"Listen, Zelda. I'll tell you this once and once only. We don't go for walkies at 5 a.m., so stop waking me up at ungodly hours. As for crapping on Mr Jeremy's front porch, I can only ask you to take your business elsewhere. I don't like him either, but we must try and be good neighbours."

The lack of exercise might become a problem for the dog, with all those scraps being brought home from McDonald's. It is preferred that Whippets remain lean and mean. They're not as quick as greyhounds but like to think they are.

Everybody at the Scottish restaurant liked the four-legged fireball and spoiled her rotten. Of course, the health and safety people would not have been thrilled about having a canine only a sniff and a snort away from a Happy Meal, but what they didn't know wouldn't hurt them. What management didn't know would be another thing. Tash took so much product home she never needed to invest in dog food from the supermarket.

When the long-awaited promotion came, the lady graduated from the onion department to housekeeping. There were tables to be cleared and toilets to be cleaned—a dirty job, but somebody had to do it. The surprise apparition appeared on her second day in new surroundings when she ran into an old client by the name of Gus Clutterbuck, who arrived with a wife and three kids in tow. Gus was a Cub leader and, for a while, president of the Mother Teresa Foundation, a community initiative promoting love and hope.

Natasha remembered him as her Tuesday man when retribution pain would be the first cab off the rank, followed by jailhouse justice and the rack, just for the fun of it. She would then send him back to his family, full of remorse and remedial regret. It might have had something to do with those Boy Scouts.

Gus ordered beetroot with his burger, which blended in with his red face, ever so obvious when he spotted Madam Lash wiping down the tables. In situations like this, professionalism takes over, and the quick-thinking fellow herded the kids out the door, offering to bring their meals out to the car. Natasha gave him a wink as he departed.

Even with her income flow reduced, life in London proved to be more than acceptable for the native of Odessa. Everybody was so friendly, especially the men. Somehow, she managed to educate Zelda, and they walked regular hours through Hyde Park and other green areas around Kensington and Chelsea. I don't like to say this, but the woman needed education herself. She was not a person who picked up after her pet, which would shame her if this should become public knowledge. Making matters worse, the dog acquired this habit of wanting to crap on people's porches. David Beckham, Elton John, and Robbie Williams all opened their front doors to discover a present from you-know-who.

If the frisky friend was disappointed in her walking pal, it was because she didn't play ball. The animal loved fetch, but because of Tash's lack of enthusiasm, the Whippet gate-crashed the games of others, and they didn't like it. The fastest is always first to the retrievable object. This caused friction between owners and participants, but it stopped after the harrier from Holland Park took on a Pit Bull from Paddington. Too much to bear, I'm afraid. Zelda and her mistress didn't leave the house for forty-eight hours.

The incentive for Natasha to rejoin the world was the news that she had been promoted to manager of her fast food outlet. Although her underlings were only girls and boys, this return to power exhilarated her, a feeling not experienced since her dungeon days. Nat always enjoyed her dominance over men, but now she could also move against some of those petulant young drama queens who thought they knew it all. Her appointment was popular with management, who thought they had acquired the complete package, with the Whippet being such a cheap waste disposal unit.

The magnificent mutt, with all her faults, was a party animal and possessed this extraordinary capacity to recognise fellow travellers. One morning, during walkies, the comfortable couple came across this rather scruffy character seated on a bench and feeding the pigeons. Or poisoning them? The dog chose to intervene.

One would guess Zelda thought there would be a treat in his pocket for her, but unfortunately not. The pat on the head more or less confirmed the stranger as a friend for life, so Natasha sat down beside the chap and discovered that the poor guy had lost his job. How sad.

At the best of times, Odessa and other southern Ukraine towns were awash with politics, so when the youngster set foot in the UK, her interest moved in other directions. She avoided the daily tabloids and concentrated her attention on fashion magazines and the antics of celebrities on Twitter and TikTok. Otherwise, she may have recognised a former prime minister of her adopted country.

Zelda recognised the aroma of dog on his person, and she wasn't wrong. The character did own a Jack Russell, presently in custody for urinating in a woman's handbag. Can you believe it?

The new manager pondered the possibility of finding room in her budget to employ another onion slicer, only until the poor chap could get back on his feet, and he would have to present for a haircut. The pigeons interrupted her thoughts by attacking the said gentleman, with the dog coming to his rescue with her gut-wrenching bark. Tash leapt up to help shoo them away, and when she turned around, she noticed the stranger shuffling off down the path like a pensioner on a promise.

Even though she was faster than a flying sausage, the Whippet always stopped to smell the roses (and anything else worth investigating), and she made new friends easily. Natasha, less satisfied, missed her former clients, so she decided to re-open the dungeon for selected customers, confident she would be able to maintain two careers at the same time.

She searched her flat for those brochures that served her so well in the past. In light of recent events, distribution would be limited. Having found the glossies, and the mailing list, the woman put a line through several former clients, currently hog-tied by royal commitments.

This salacious activity would be new to Zelda, who, to date, had shared her mistress with no one. There would need to be a little softening up because jealousy might rear its ugly head, and who wanted that?

"You'll love the cabinet minister, Zed. He's a little obese but possesses a great sense of humour and always brings gifts. He'll bring some treats for you if you're friendly. You will be friendly, won't you?"

The person she talked about was the Foreign Minister and the first of the "old team" to reappear. However, this would be a night like no other. He arrived a little dishevelled, but carrying a Fortnum & Mason Delight Box for Dogs.

How did he know I now have a pet? thought the lady in a leotard.

After the initial greeting and a small aperitif, the punishment session began, but Madam Lash realised something was wrong with her visitor.

His normal ruddy complexion had taken on a ghastly pallor not seen before, and he slurred his words.

"Are you alright? You don't look well."

"I've been stab…stabbed by a Russian with an umbrella."

"No!" she cried, astonished and slightly bemused.

"How did you know the brute came from the Soviet Union?"

"The canopy didn't open….poison tip. I don't have long…long for this world. I must confess something to you before I leave."

The girl was stunned.

Is this what people in Britain call an April Fools' joke?

You couldn't blame her for thinking that. Nevertheless, Nat let him have his say, as he wanted to unburden himself of his secret.

"I have been deceiving you, Natasha. I do not enjoy pain and have been attending your sessions just to keep an eye on you. Your safety is my responsibility."

There is no point in recording the girl's response because it was a Slavic swear word. She allowed him to continue but with growing concern and suspicion.

"You believe your father is dead, but this is not so. He is an MI6 operative living in deep cover in Moscow. He remains a thorn in the side of Vladimir Putin and is a wanted man. In order to protect you, he arranged for you to be spir-spirited out of Odessa, and we h-h-hid you in the safest house we knew—the convent."

The man's face, now quite contorted, indicated the high level of pain he must have been suffering. A wisp of blood appeared on his lower lip. Natasha stared at him as if he were an alien.

"We have paid for your education and the rental of this flat. As I said, you are our responsibility."

"This is not true," said the girl. "I pay my own rent."

"I'm afraid you have no idea how much accommodation costs in this area. We bridge the gap and do so wil-willingly."

The Foreign Minister tried to rise from his chair, and she helped him. Such a large man; she hoped he wouldn't fall on top of her. This type of thing can be embarrassing.

"I should call an ambulance. You are very sick."

"Thank you, child, but not today. My situation is ter-terminal. I must not be found on your premises. Do you have a sharp knife?"

Can a dog bark? Every hooker in London carries a sharp knife, with Nat no exception. He wanted her to remove his jacket and slice open his shirt near the shoulder blade.

"There is a microchip embedded in my shoulder. I want you to cut it out and keep it. The chip contains all the information you want to know about your father. If the Russkies find it, you will never see your father again."

My God, thought Tash. This has to be a movie. I don't believe what's happening.

"OK, Mr Spy Man, but how do I read a microchip?"

As the visitor dragged himself towards the door, a sly grin appeared on his face. He had now introduced Madam Lash into the world of espionage and clandestine encounters, and she appeared ready for it.

"There is one person at MI6 who will help you. His name is Ja-Ja-James."

"James Bond! You're hooking me up with James Bond?"

"I'm afraid not, my dear. His name is James Dibbledick."

Zelda, who was still ravaging the Delight Box, stopped eating, raised her head and looked at her mistress. She then returned to the Fortnum & Mason box of treats. One and all looked forward to meeting James Dibbledick.

"He is a fine chap," said the government man. "Very reliable, but if he takes you to dinner, don't let him order the wine. The fellow is a cheapskate."

Again, the dying man refused a call for medical assistance and asked to be helped up the stairs. The last Natasha saw of him, he was limping down the street, trying to get as far away from her abode as possible.

For once in her life, the woman viewed the morning news and discovered the wounded warrior had managed to walk three blocks. A jogger found him dead on the pavement, but the report ended there, with no mention of his credentials or bleeding shoulder. Neither was the cause of death reported.

Let me put your mind at rest. The pride of Vauxhall Cross was not one of the Dibbledicks from Doncaster, who dabbled in disinformation, destabilisation, and deceit. Energetic and enthusiastic, with an engaging smile, James possessed an agreeable disposition, and he always made agitated people feel comfortable.

The intelligence agent was no athlete, but he didn't carry any surplus weight. The woman sitting opposite him considered the young man to be about average height for a spy, and she did note him to be quite handsome; but you think that about anyone with blond hair, don't you?

"Thank you, Natasha, for bringing me this microchip. I will have it decoded and advise you of any of the contents relating to your father. Any classified information will be withheld. You understand, don't you?"

Of course she understood, old chum. Since Sir Eric spilled his guts prior to his unfortunate demise, she now classified herself as a fully-fledged member of the Spies R Us brigade. They did let her into the building, didn't they?

Some people may be impressed that anyone could track down one of Britain's most elusive undercover men in such a short time. The poppet just presented at the front desk and asked for him by name. Zelda didn't make it past security. Unless you are a police dog, they make few allowances. Years earlier, two puppies called Ko and Kane embarrassed the customs people, and they have never lived it down.

"I have not seen my father since I was very young," explained the visitor, sitting on the end of her chair and breathing in all the atmosphere and ambience of the super-spy's personal domain.

"Do you know him?"

The super-spy produced his most charming smile as he deposited the microchip in his top drawer.

"I certainly do. He used to be one of my instructors at training school. I can't tell you much about that, but I do want you to know he is highly thought of within these walls. However, I was unaware he maintained a relationship with Sir Eric, and I'm surprised that someone with such seniority had a chip on his shoulder.

When Natasha collected her dog and left the premises, she was oblivious to the degree of scrutiny imposed from above. From his office on the fifth floor, her new-found friend followed her departure with concern, worried about her safety. Over recent months, five visitors to Vauxhall Cross had died within days of their visit, and, in his business, coincidence is always your last consideration.

He couldn't help but think that the pooch on the lead was taking her for a walk, but there didn't appear to be a tail, so perhaps his anxiety might be unwarranted. He continued his window watch until they both disappeared along The Embankment. Unbeknown to the spook, their destination was a bus stop Tash knew well. With midday approaching, thoughts turned to lunch, and Natasha loved eating al fresco in South Kensington. So did her companion, but she enjoyed eating anywhere.

While standing in line for the transport to arrive, the hungry hooker became conscious of a sharp pull on her lead. Her charge, having discovered a point of interest just a few metres away from the bus stop, wanted a closer look at the contemporary butcher shop, new to that address.

The magnificent skyscraper neared completion, with the ground floor shops already rented and open for business. Furnishings and appliances were being transferred to the 24th level the easy way—by high-rise crane. Although she knew she would lose her position in the queue, the dog owner allowed herself to be dragged to the store frontage of Coronation Butchers—by appointment to Buckingham Palace. Zelda balanced on her rear haunches and stood at the window, drooling over the meat display. A person bound for Pimlico, who claimed Natasha's vacated place in the line, couldn't help but laugh at the absurdity of the situation. She would never laugh again.

Those bathroom fittings on their way to the 24th floor had been poorly packed, and one of the side panels broke. The Swedish-designed bidet had nowhere to go but down, and down it went. What can I say? It was ugly, and it took all day to clean up the mess. The "Old Bill" interviewed everyone in the vicinity, and Natasha found it hard to concentrate. She should have been the victim.

"I won't take much of your time, madam. The deceased came from Italy—Genoa."

"No, I didn't know her, but we did have a short conversation. She liked my Zelda. The woman moved here six months ago and immediately purchased a rescue dog for a tenner. His name is Pavarotti."

The constable was not a music lover, so this extraneous detail went unrecorded. Tash went over to the curb and threw up. All told, it would be a day one hoped to forget. Nevertheless, she was impressed with Mr. Dibbledick and looked forward to whatever knowledge he might acquire concerning her father.

The contents of the microchip were revealing, but contained little intelligence about Kostos, Natasha's father. He was the guy who put it all together, the man who maintained a mole in the military. James Dibbledick recognised co-ordinates for missile sites, army barracks, and even Putin's country dacha. The names and addresses of all the generals were listed, as well as certain spies operating in the West. No wonder the communists wanted to acquire the chip.

The secret service man wondered why the Foreign Secretary chose to use Natasha as his conduit to MI6, given there was limited material of a personal nature on the microchip. Then all appeared obvious. Sir Eric didn't trust the contact he met weekly, the head of their agency and gatekeeper to a thousand secrets.

The head of this organisation used to be called M. That person is now recognised as B (Boss), and the current appointee is one, Boris Borscht. Eyebrows must have been raised when this appointment was made. With the war in Ukraine in full swing, the only UK parliamentarian allowed to travel to Russia is the Foreign Secretary, on a peacekeeping mission.

How Kostos located facilities to insert the microchip is anyone's guess, but he did, and it came to pass that a Cabinet Minister found himself operating as a covert agent—exciting but foolhardy. The relationship with MI6's Special K must have been pretty strong because he fulfilled his promise to guard and protect the vulnerable daughter until his untimely death. It is not known whether he advised Kostos that Daddy's pride and joy was a hooker.

"I am not a hooker," explained Tash, throwing a quick glance at Miss Judgemental, quietly sitting by her feet near the chopping board. The caring pet owner prepared the pooch's dinner as if it were her own, and the large, juicy Coronation sausage looked really appetising. Natasha had purchased a few extra porkers for herself.

I know you are asking, "How could they eat after the trauma they've just gone through?"

Yes, having to hang around for those police interviews made a difficult day even more frustrating. Zelda had her heart set on a visit to the butcher with palace connections, and who would deny her? Let's face it. If their delicacies were good enough for the Royal Corgis, they would be good enough for Speedy Gonzalez from Holland Park.

Natasha couldn't stop thinking about the dead woman who replaced her in the queue. The least she could do was buy a bottle of chianti and toast her journey into the afterlife. Then there were the ones left behind. What would happen to poor Pavarotti, the ten-pound rescue dog?

The late mail delivery gave Tash something to think about while eating her bangers and mash. She received an invitation to attend the annual cricket match between "The Pigs" and "The Bulldogs."

Every year, the police and MI6 lock horns in a struggle for bragging rights. On this occasion, the game would be played in Turnham Green, but with no specific instructions to assist a first-timer in finding the oval. Natasha presumed the invite was down to her contact at Vauxhall Cross, who would probably bring with him a report on the microchip. The competing sides were listed on the invitation, with one of her best customers elected team captain.

The chief constable would open the batting for his side, but the opposition might have been a little short on talent. James Dibbledick would bat, bowl, and also be the designated wicketkeeper. The Australian ambassador would be one of the umpires, and Gordon Ramsay won the catering gig, reporting to Boris Borscht.

Natasha came from Ukraine, so she didn't understand cricket. Nevertheless, if it involved guys with balls, who wanted to bowl a maiden over, she would be ready to learn. What would she wear? Would they welcome Zelda as an escort?

"Hey, Zed, do you want to play fetch with some cool dudes?"

🐾

Because the Doncaster Dibbledicks didn't have a very good reputation, the London namesake was happy to accept the august appellation his peers bestowed on him—James Blond. One should confirm his locks as natural and not coloured from a bottle.

The man in question studied the microfilm a number of times with a magnifying glass. There was valuable information recorded, but none of it pointed to a top-level turn-coat in the organisation, and yet the Foreign Secretary's actions seemed to indicate just that. He raised his eyes to the bookshelf in the corner of the room, which contained every volume John le Carré had ever written. The head of MI6, Boris Borscht, possessed a similar library, so whatever entrapment James Blond might instigate would have to be not only novel but indisputable. The fact that the man ate Blini and Kasha for breakfast might just be discontentment with English food.

At the last moment, prior to leaving for the cricket match, James confessed to his boss that Tash was the source of the microfilm and that she possessed intelligence regarding a mole in the agency. This wasn't true, but what is a white lie in a world of darkness and deception?

"When is she going to further confide in you?" asked the insidious infiltrator as they waited for the elevator.

"I've invited her to our cricket match today."

One can always anticipate the arrival of the lift at MI6 headquarters. There is a whirring noise followed by a couple of chugs. Before the doors opened, Boris produced an excellent affectation of a thought bomb.

"Hold the elevator, James. I've forgotten my umbrella."

It would only be a forty-second delay, but enough for the intelligence agent to contemplate and reason. Looking out the window, he observed a beautiful sunny day, but the brolly in question was no parasol.

When the chief constable cut the ball to the boundary to bring up his fifty, muted applause came from those in the easy chairs in front of the pavilion. The woman sitting alone with her dog was more appreciative. She shouted and whistled, and the man bowed in appreciation. Of course, he couldn't identify the lass under her hat. Perhaps he wouldn't have recognised her anyway without a whip and leather restraints.

James Dibbledick positioned his friend near the toilet block because he could hide a couple of operatives there, who would not be seen from the pavilion. His instructions to Tash were to be friendly with everyone but be wary if approached by a man with an umbrella. That man would be a double agent. The gal, with a can of mace within reach, didn't see herself as expendable.

Natasha was up for all of this because of a recent rethink. Perhaps the owner of the brutal brolly that killed her client was not a KGB type who returned to Moscow, but the man joshing with Gordon Ramsay, Boris Borscht. They say revenge is best served cold.

The chef employed staff to pass around the canapés, but it looked like Boris would take it upon himself to carry some appetisers over to the lady sitting by herself. With his umbrella hanging from his arm, he moved in her direction, unaware that James Blond was talking into his shoulder from his position behind the stumps.

"I noticed you over here by yourself and thought you might like to try some of Gordon's fabulous fare."

The growl from near his feet indicated that another party might be interested in the food, but the visitor ignored the dog and placed the plate in front of the hapless hooker, who reached forward with one hand and back with another. Gripping the mace tightly, she would be ready for whatever might come next.

The villainous fiend would never go at her with an all-out attack with so many people around. A little prick was required, and Nat could see him edging the umbrella towards her bare arm. Time and tide wait for no man...or woman. She unleashed the mace, and he screamed like a pig, clutching at his face. The agents hiding in the toilets pounced, as a loud roar came from the pavilion. The chief constable had just been bowled out for a well-made seventy-one.

It's a shame John le Carré is no longer with us because I believe he would have liked this story, although I expect he would have changed the hero's surname. After all, he switched his own name from Cornwell to something Gallic (not garlic).

I haven't told you what happened to the double agent because there is the possibility of a mini-series. Nevertheless, the poison pouch they found in the umbrella proved incriminating. I also neglected to consummate a romance between the lead characters because I have many underage readers, and I don't want to infer that sex with a professional is romantic. Nor did I wish to enlarge on any of Zelda's less endearing features. The bitch is a bloody nymphomaniac.

THE SNAKE IN THE GRASS FROM BOULDER PASS

The western wind blew the tumbleweeds into the parched patch of planet that was the only street of Big Rock, a town without charm or dignity. The days were so hot, nothing or no one moved faster than the pianola roll at the local saloon, the only entertainment outlet in the territory, a situation which embarrassed many.

Boot Hill Boulevard didn't go anywhere because of this gigantic hill of granite in the way, towering over the community like a doting parent. The thoroughfare started at the cemetery and the last building on the cusp of nowhere was the county jail, where all new arrivals were required to present their credentials to the sheriff. Sally O'Gorman, the first woman in the state to carry such a badge, wore it with courage and conviction, setting a fine example for those who supported her ideals and principles, including her dog Billy, aka the K9 Kid.

Deputy Billy had been empowered by the visiting marshal, Fleck Gunderson, who authorised the stipend of four packets of Kit Carson Kibble per week, with accommodation provided in the corner of the office. However, Billy's entitlement didn't permit him to become a member of the peacekeeper's union.

Marshal Gunderson only stopped by when trouble presented, which disappointed Sally, him being drop-dead gorgeous and quick on the draw. Most of his adversaries dropped dead, and then he would be gone.

"It may be some time before I come this way again, sweet lips," said the uncomplicated lawman, casually roping up a captive destined for three years in the state pen.

"If you two want to be alone, I can wait outside," suggested the prisoner, hoping like hell that his gang would be outside and ready to rescue him. The reply came from the dog—a deep-throated growl.

Where do they get these animals from?, thought the recalcitrant rustler. His experience with Texas Heelers proved far less confrontational. They were pussies compared to this cur.

✦

The history of the Old West is littered with tales of derring-do but light on for women warriors. Annie Oakley made the cut, and Calamity Jane caused such a commotion, they also included her. We are all familiar with the Gunfight at the OK Corral, but what about the Bunfight at the BR Bakery? The perfumed peacemaker couldn't have been more impressive, with her dog riding shotgun.

The bakery in this town is an institution. The first loaves came out of the oven at around 5.30 a.m., with at least one customer ready and waiting. Julie McHarg had five hungry mouths to feed every day at her boarding house. At 9 a.m., the establishment transformed into tea rooms, always well patronised. The rolls and buns arrived on the midday tray, and even the Mexicans seemed interested. Then the out-of-towners turned up.

Hamburger Hill is smaller than Big Rock and cut off from the rest of the world. The nearest stagecoach stop at Macy's Trading Post offered an avenue to wider horizons but some fifty miles away. Boot Hill Boulevard became a magnet for thrill-seekers, being the Bourbon Street of its day. The tea rooms always proved popular, although animosity often arose between the locals and the visitors. In this instance, disparaging remarks offended, and all hell broke loose.

How many people were shot in the eye with currants or received a shortcrust to the belly? There was flour everywhere. The master baker, a beast, understood more about life than yeast. Karate hadn't been invented, but the brute displayed all the moves. Sally arrived after much blood had been spilt, and regaining control proved difficult. Jacob Hoffman had mobilised the bagel brigade, but the Danish couple from Hamburger Hill would not be denied. Chaos reigned.

The K9 Kid had experienced bar room brawls before, and rounding up people is not too different to rounding up cattle. You run the perimeter of the mob and dart in and bite ankles when necessary. In truth, this scrap petered out because of exhaustion, with too many pie-eaters on the front line. The sheriff foresaw a substantial damage bill and didn't want to exacerbate the situation by arresting anybody. So, she assembled everybody and led the chorus in a rousing rendition of "We Shall Overcome." Law enforcement often involves public relations initiatives.

The summer proved difficult for the first lady of law and order. She missed the magnetic marshal, and what about those friends who ended up on Boot Hill, including the local cobbler, who always knew how to fit spurs that jingle-jangled; his line of R.M. Williams footwear from Australia always exceeded expectations. Billy also felt a bit jaded from the hot weather and kept encountering other creatures who tried to find shade in town, mostly scorpions and rattlesnakes.

This brings me to the focus of this fascinating yarn—The Snake in the Grass from Boulder Pass.

You're going to ask, so I'll tell you. Boulder Pass is halfway between Little Rock and Big Rock in Arkansas. It is not in Illinois or Virginia and nowhere near Pebble Beach.

Snatch Bilious claimed to be a self-made man, and who would dispute such an assertion? He made up his name, his employment background, and his marital status. The guy was quite photogenic, with his picture adorning the walls of many community buildings, including the post office and the sheriff's office.

Who or what encouraged the outcast to come to this hideaway in Hicksville? Well, this much is known. Pat Garrett ran him out of half-a-dozen towns in New Mexico and may have alerted the authorities in Boulder Pass of his presence in their region.

Moving into a news-deprived neighbourhood made sense. These folks thought James Garfield was still president, but they weren't stupid. The traders in town tended to ignore the fact that money is the root of all evil and would have designs on his Pony Express Gold Card. No one knew better than this sadistic stick-up man about the roots of all evil.

As the outrageous outlaw trundled up Boot Hill Boulevard, the thermometer indicated a hundred and ten degrees Fahrenheit. Even the tamales in town were in tears, not to mention his horse. The pianola player at the saloon had taken a turn for the worse, but the desk clerk prevailed and checked him in under difficult circumstances. He gave the fellow a room in the west wing, which supposedly collected the evening breeze at twilight time. There hadn't been an evening breeze since 1851.

It didn't go unnoticed that the recent arrival failed to register his presence as required, but the uncomfortable heat might be an acceptable excuse. Billy was sent over to the den of inequity to investigate. The wily animal never entered through the swinging front doors but via the kitchen, where he befriended a comrade, the larger-than-life chef Pierre Le Pont from New Orleans. On this occasion, the K9 Kid spent valuable time with his pal, leaving Mr Bilious to consult with the local representative of the Palmolive Soap Company. After a long ride in the sun, you can end up pretty smelly.

When the dog returned to the office, Sally guessed where he had been, at the same time looking forward to chow in the dining hall that night. She saw coyote stew dripping from the jowls of the dishlicker. Nevertheless, job done. The tailwagger stood up against his employer and pawed her sidearm; the visitor now identified as a gunfighter.

If you're a newbie in town, there's no chance you can sneak into the dining hall unnoticed. Those already seated stopped eating; the young waitress blinked twice, and Candles McCrory squirmed in his chair, all 6 foot. 5 inches of him. The hungry house guest surveyed each empty table before making his decision. He always liked to have his back to the wall. When comfortable, he would check out the menu.

Forget the menu because you didn't get options. As long as they retained their man mountain as cook, Chef's Choice would never be a source of criticism. Anyway, who would complain about coyote stew? Not everyone gets to sample fresh meat daily.

Sally O'Gorman walked into the room, and all conversation ceased. She ambled up to the gunslinger and waited for him to raise his eyes— probing pupils, dirty, dank, dangerous, and diabolically disturbing. The sheriff liked to think she could read people, but this encounter would be like dancing in the dark with an African American.

"Howdy, stranger. Are you in town for long?"

"What's it to you, bitch?" came the arrogant reply.

Oh, dear! Another overconfident drifter about to underestimate the town's leading law officer. The nomad from New Mexico didn't have a high opinion of women, but, in this case, he might bite off more than he could chew. Sorry for the cliché, but the rebel, about to have his dinner, dared to be still munching stale tobacco. The lady in the room may have been disgusted but remained as cool as a skunk in the moonlight—a tribute to her patience and deodorant.

"New arrivals are supposed to report to the jailhouse. I expect to see you first thing in the morning, amigo. We might have to measure your moustache. It looks a bit long to me."

The laws relating to personal hygiene irked many and continued to be controversial, but unruly hair growth needed to be monitored. Several unsavoury gentlemen from south of the border were moved on, as well as Doc Holliday and Bill Cody. Doc proved to be a great loss. Nobody knew where to go for dental care.

The woman was saved from a fate worse than death by the spittoon near the man's table. The gunslinger may have been about to say something provocative when the coyote stew arrived, diverting his attention to the cut-up carnivore, pulverised and parboiled; a banquet for the weary traveller.

The daughter of democracy backed out of the dining hall and, after a spin around the bar area, left the building, knowing things would soon spice up a bit. The "Nymphs du Prairie" hit the stage at eight o'clock, when whisky sales often doubled. Sally would send her deputy over later to check whether the clientele behaved themselves.

Some people said the dog was overworked, but he enjoyed the overtime. Many of the locals established an alliance with the panting pet and slipped him a treat now and then or a neck massage. All appreciated and well-remembered.

The relationship with the blow-in didn't start well, and you can blame it on those dark penetrating eyes. The Kid could weed out a weasel by staring unflinchingly into his baby blues, which often betrayed the desire to deceive. By the time the working dog started his round, the ladies in a line, having completed the first part of their contract, now mixed with the inebriated punters, social intercourse a given.

Not all the customers were drunk, the exception being the new guy, who balanced Belle Amoré on his knee and whispered sweet nothings in her ear. The dancer and cabaret singer had met the likes of Snatch Bilious before. She reckoned he would more than likely try and hustle her out of her bustle, so she kept a derringer in her garter. On the other hand...if he had money?

Outside, the night, dark and dangerous, masked the moon and made progress on the boardwalk difficult. It was unusually cold, and Billy rugged-up accordingly. The only building lit was the bank, which made his perimeter check a lot easier. Should there be would-be intruders in the vicinity, he would get a whiff of the varmints before chasing them out to tumbleweed territory. In the past, some mean dudes chose to stay and make a play against the deputised dog, but they came out of it second best.

All ready for the perimeter check!

Sally often recalled the day he carved his name in glory. William Bonney bounced into town, claiming to be the GOAT (greatest of all time). With the bank employees lying on the floor, Bonney rifled the safe. Billy came at him; the outlaw dropped his gun and the money and ran out of the building clutching his wrist. He managed to get on his horse and ride off, but he never came back. The GOAT in Big Rock was the K9 Kid. You had better believe it. Today, they have time locks on the vaults, but if you look at the front door of the depository, you can still read the notation—*this property is patrolled and protected by the K9 Kid.*

By the time the diminutive deputy reached the home of harmony, the horny hard man was performing a lewd act with Belle Amoré in his room in the west wing, his gun belt on the floor and her derringer in denial. The dog settled down beside the entrance to the Honeymoon Suite and hoped they would be quiet, at least until breakfast.

The Last Chance Saloon, cabaret nightly, was also an institution. Some folks remembered other saloons during the gold rush, but with those days long gone, no semblance of competition or propriety remained. The girls were hot, and so was the beer. In later years, the same whiskey would be used to fuel horseless carriages. You now understand where the term "rotgut" originated.

People who went to church stayed at Julie McHarg's boarding house. The rest bedded down at the Last Chance, with many possibilities. Should you want to be near your horse, a ground floor room might be available, with easy access to Patrick Carey's stables, grooming extra, and water at competitive prices.

The arse from Boulder Pass relaxed in a deluxe room on the second level, but some doubt existed as to who might pay for it. Visitors of similar ilk often requested consideration, until after they robbed the bank. Of course, we're talking pre-Sally times. She impressed during the bunfight, but the lady could be just as capable in a gunfight. The faithful friend added a touch of solidity to the partnership, and only fools would underestimate them. Mr Bilious wasn't a fool, but he needed to lift his game. He misjudged Pat Garrett, as did many others (refer William Bonney).

The gentleman in question also tended to be insolent and defiant, which is why this particular amigo had no intention of registering at the sheriff's office that morning. It didn't matter. The resident law person slept in, which meant Billy would serve breakfast to the prisoners, one banana at a time.

At Mrs McHarg's boarding rooms, the hostess provided beans for breakfast (and lunch and dinner) and instructed all guests to smoke their pipes and cheroots on the verandah. The air in the dining room after supper could be volatile. Oversleep and there would be no brekky-in-bed unless you wore a sheriff's badge. The female residents always tried to look after each other. Where else did the suggestion come from that perhaps someone might be overworked and needed rest? In those days, the concept of a six-day working week was not a concept at all.

"Really, Sally, I know you won't hear a word against Fleck, but he has to send you some help. This town is getting bigger by the day, and how will you ever find a husband if you have no time off?"

The woman projected a pertinent point. The sheriff met a lot of men, most of them behind bars. The new arrival looked promising, but he was rude and didn't respect women. Nobody wants to marry someone like that. The smart money supported Gunderson as the guy, but tittle-tattle from Texas to Tombstone indicated he might sign up with Wild Bill Hickok's travelling show. Annie Oakley, already on this tour, enjoyed a reputation as a renowned man-eater, and the marshal might be easy prey.

Sally managed to dress while cradling her steaming cup of coffee, then gulped down her beans and headed for the office, now in some kind of state. Billy couldn't transport the beverages as well as the bananas. Candles McCrory, in on a drunk and disorderly charge, looked the least fearsome of the prisoners, so she invoked executive privilege.

"Hey, Candles, here's the mop. Clean up the mess, and I'll give you your freedom."

The woman was so versatile, a free thinker who always managed to overcome situations in a most positive manner. At this time, she couldn't waste her energy on domestic chores. The gal anticipated bigger issues and reckoned they would involve Snatch Bilious.

Two other members of his gang entered the town within minutes of each other, and they both looked mean and ornery. Surely, onlookers might have observed their empty saddlebags and wondered why.

When the bank manager crossed the road for lunch in the saloon, he couldn't anticipate that he would be dining with three desperadoes, famous and fearsome, with a price on their heads for many unspeakable acts. They were seated at another table, speaking in whispers, while enjoying the *plat du jour*—coyote brains, a small but otherwise tasty meal. Their leader let them begin to appreciate their grub before attending to business.

"My friends, this is going to be easy," said the scary strategist, lowering his voice to be almost inaudible.

"The law is a woman and she only has a pooch for backup. I want you guys to stop gorging yourselves and ask for a doggie bag. We'll dump it outside the adjoining building and test his priorities."

"Gee, Snake, we haven't eaten since yesterday. Are you sure?"

Jake Smudge didn't often question his boss and now regretted doing it. The answer was not what he wanted to hear.

"Do you want a bite on the bum or a tidy sum? We're going to conduct a robbery, Jake, old pal. We do it my way."

You may have noticed that one of the important characters in this absorbing tale has been addressed in a rather intimate way, a name not recognised by most god-fearing, law-abiding people.

It is a deserved sobriquet because this burly brigand pioneered violence-free bank robberies. His modus operandi involved entering secure premises and tossing a rattlesnake into the teller's cage. The staff would bolt out of the building, allowing him to help himself. In time, he graduated to a Colt .45 as his weapon of choice and used dynamite on occasions, but to the purveyors of tabloid hyperbole, Snake and his sidekick Jake grabbed all the headlines.

Some people in Arkansas can't see the woods for the trees. Benjamin Tightwad, the bank manager, received copies of all "Wanted" notices and yet failed to spot one of the most notorious outlaws in the country, sitting opposite him. As the three cowboys rose to leave, a moment of vague recollection surfaced from within. This brought a frown to his face and the incentive to summon the waitress.

"Juanita, one of those gentlemen who left, his face is familiar."

"Yes, Mr Tightwad, that's Snatch Bilious, the bank robber."

Oops, not another broken coffee cup? The loan arranger flew out of his chair before you could say Kemosabe. He covered the wide expanse of Boot Hill Boulevard in record time and arrived back in his office, panting like a porcupine on a pushbike. The poster on his whiteboard confirmed what the waitress told him. However, no unauthorised withdrawals had been made. He breathed a sigh of relief and penned a note to the sheriff, to be delivered by the junior accounts clerk, renowned for his sloppiness and lack of attention to detail.

The lad obtained his position because of the intercession of Fleck Gunderson, who insisted on helping rehome former inmates of youth detention institutions. The guy was such a goody two-shoes, it sickened some people, and putting one of these reprobates anywhere near money would be plain dumb; not that anyone would accuse Fleck of being dumb.

The young man would say later that he couldn't find Sally and thought she might be in the saloon. He couldn't explain why his search in that particular venue lasted for three hours. This is where he acquired some new friends during his bar sojourn, all interested in his line of employment and the layout of his workplace. One of them offered to deliver his note for him. After all, the lad looked a bit unsteady on his feet.

Not all transmissions remained undelivered. Single Sally, undermanned in so many ways, thought her deputy might be doubtful value in a gunfight, so she managed to send a telegram to Fleck, advising him of the presence of wanted men in his jurisdiction. The failure to receive Tightwad's note proved a good thing, as she didn't have to react immediately, and the passage of time suited all parties to the inevitable confrontation. Snatch, in particular, leaned over the map the youngster had drawn for him. He explained the plan to his sidekicks.

"We'll go in through the back door and out through the front. It's a matter of loading the saddlebags and riding out of town. I'll leave an IOU with the desk clerk for our accommodation."

That night, the same man attempted to leave an IOU with Belle Amoré, but she would have none of it. An altercation followed with words spoken. The mongrel slapped her, which is what you don't do with this gal. He received a kick in the goolies for his trouble, and she stormed out of the room.

"Damn," said the snake in the grass. "The bitch knows about the robbery. If she interferes, I swear I'll kill her."

Dancing girls can look after themselves. They have to. They don't call it the Wild West for nothing. The troupe, known as the "Nymphs du Prairie," all boasted experience in hand-to-hand fighting, and most of them passed muster on the rifle range. Although not advertised, a gun room in the bowels of the hotel contained a small arsenal. One never knew when the premises might be under threat.

Neither did anyone know that Sally received a visit from Belle early next morning while having breakfast at the boarding house. Good timing—the table groaned under the pile of flapjacks, dripping with honey and hayseed. A little later, over at the saloon, observant people saw the K9 Kid hovering around those swinging doors, an indication he might be following someone.

Can I tell you what I know? The raid on the bank would be set for midday—high noon. The sun would be high and energy low; certainly, nobody in the money mansion would have the capacity to out-draw the fugitive thief. Jake would tether the horses outside the premises and come in through the front door while the other two entered by the rear entrance. The whole heist, expected to take fifteen minutes, would see them with a similar break over the posse if Sally managed to recruit in the aftermath of the robbery. What could go wrong?

"This is a stick-up, my friends. Raise your hands and walk into the centre of the room. You too, fat man. I'm not going to miss such a belly, am I?"

Jake appeared to be confident, as there were no customers, and the only other employee tried to sneak out the back as the other two came in. From then on, they didn't talk much, just nodded to each other as the teller stuffed saddlebags with low-denomination cash. It is hard to confirm whether the intern recognised his drinking buddies, with their faces covered, but he must have identified Snake because the chap possessed a distinctive voice.

"Now, let's open the vault, Mr Manager. And we haven't got all day."

Credit where credit is due. Benjamin Tightwad, the loan arranger, showed no signs of distress and appeared happy to stand up to these bullies.

"It's open. Help yourselves. Or are you looking for money?"

Was the gun-toting cowboy confused? You bet. He walked into the vault and then returned, alarmed and antagonistic.

"There's no money."

"Exactly," said the portly prince of the paradox. "We're a bank with little money and no longer safeguard our seed security here. Because you plundering pigs keep robbing us, we have come to a better arrangement."

"Which is?" demanded the outlaw.

"We store the cash in the jailhouse."

Jake and Snake looked at each other, and the three of them ran for the door, but they didn't reach their horses.

Standing in a semi-circle by the entrance were five exotic dancers, all brandishing Winchester rifles. Coming in from beside the robbers was the sheriff, also carrying.

"C'mon, boys. Hands high and no quick moves. Belle, in particular, is a crack shot, and the dog is an ankle-biter."

I don't want you to think this yarn is all about liberated women, but you have to take your hat off to the girls. They enjoyed cuffing the captives and marching them off to confinement. The prisoners were all charged and processed by the time Fleck Gunderson arrived following Sally's SOS.

The good news for lovers of pulp fiction is that the hunk agreed to stay and, on the back of a loan from Mr Tightwad, purchased a small holding not far out of town. Fleck and Sally married in the fall, with the temperature only one hundred and five degrees. The reception, held at the Last Chance Saloon, delighted all who attended, and the guests feasted on beef buffalo, caramelised coyote, and chili bean custard, all washed down with rotgut whisky and warm beer.

One of the major topics of conversation at the knees-up concerned the rumour that Wells Fargo might decide to include their town on their stagecoach route. Wow! This would really put Rocky on the map.

In reality, this didn't happen, as the people of Little Rock, suffering from an inferiority complex, lobbied their political representative to maintain the status quo. To this day, you will not find Big Rock, Arkansas, on any map.

In terms of the robbers, they must have been so frustrated, being placed in Cell J at Sally's jailhouse. Mr Tightwad had been right. Their seed capital of $9,000 lay piled in a trunk beneath the bunk of Cell K, the accommodation destination for the drunk and disorderly, with the key under Billy's mat. That's why they called him the K9 Kid.

DOG ON A LOG

Australia is a land of sweeping plains and constant rains. If those rains fall on flood-prone areas, the whole landscape changes; some folks remember the floods of '55, '86, and 2011. I can hardly remember my last bath, but I do know the rivers can overflow overnight. Just ask Rocky.

Rocky was my neighbour's dog—as big as a battleship and twice as slow. Nevertheless, a Rottweiler always demands respect. Ron had been a waiter at the city's finest restaurant, and his companion wanted for nothing. He dined better than I did. When the dynamic duo moved to the country, man's best friend took his appetite with him and adapted to his new surroundings.

Being a wise waiter, Ron managed to sell his property well, allowing him to buy a nice house by the river. He may have been surprised at the good deal he negotiated, but then again, he was unaware of the floods of '55, '86, and 2011. The city pooch wasn't even aware of the concept of a flood; otherwise, he wouldn't have chosen one of those riverside logs as his favourite resting place. Sure, his kennel had been transported up north with Ron's goods and chattels, but the verandah can be muggy on a hot night.

Have I mentioned the mutt's capacity to sleep? He napped anywhere. Those morning runs with his master were rather punishing, so you couldn't blame him for being tired most of the time. The fitness fanatic pushed himself to the limits and had longer legs than the Rottweiler. Rocky's ability to slumber was legendary. Who can forget his appearance at the community centre for the high school brass band recital? The comatose canine slept through the whole performance and snored louder than the tuba. At home, the bugger snoozed through two break-ins and the Prime Minister's Address to the Nation.

When it rained continually for days, local people expected the river to rise, but Rocky was not yet "local people." He enjoyed lying on that log and dreaming of the black and white St. Bernard up the road. Chubbs had an attractive mistress and the schemer might have been trying to formulate some kind of double date situation to accommodate Ron's carnal desires.

Chubbs and the sweet chick!

When the dreamer awoke, he found himself drifting at speed in the middle of a raging torrent. Faster than a thoroughbred I had recently supported at Flemington. To make things worse, he travelled backwards. On the credit side, he saw some animals afloat with no visible means of support. Mrs Hanneberry's long-haired llama passed by with an incredulous look on its face.

The dog, having seen Ron kayaking with his mates, had always shown interest in participating. Not anymore. This was terrifying. Too scared to try and stand up, he remained low on the bark, thinking that this reverse position sucked. Who cares where you've been? It's where you're going that matters.

In this instance, he unwittingly headed for Viagra Falls, the largest natural water catchment in the area. Thank God he couldn't see where he was going.

There are a raft of reasons why I say this, but the dog only needed to ponder one pertinent fact. The drop to the bottom from the crest was scary, and no one had ever survived such a descent due to the clump of rocks under the cascade, a permanent hazard. Should someone project themselves beyond these rocks, the depth of the plunge pool might save them.

Rocky only had moments to consider his plan of action. A few seconds before reaching the tipping point, his conveyance slammed into a tree branch in the middle of the river and turned around. As it went over the edge, he jumped.

Australia has produced several diving champions, and I doubt any of them would find fault with the Rottweiler's style, execution, and entry into the water. He nailed it. The difficulty arose when the dog emerged from the deep, as he couldn't swim. Should you expect more from a city animal? Rocky learnt quickly but breathed a sigh of relief at the sudden appearance of his former transport option, duly recognised by others as the lower half of a Eucalyptus tree trunk.

Reunited with this facility, what else could he do but go with the flow? The pool below was not as free-flowing as the surge above, but the dog and his log headed south. There were always a lot of adventures to be had down south.

🐾

In this part of the world, you don't get better Sunday afternoon entertainment than that provided by the Showboat Queen, a Mississippi paddle steamer that had not left its mooring in five years. When purchasing the "old girl," the new owners anticipated that the male community members would be seduced by the gambling tables, allowing their wives to attend the variety shows, which often included a local yodeller and a barbershop quartet. The gaming hall offered roulette, blackjack, and dice, and you would have to say this was indeed a floating crap game.

Rocky observed the whole box and dice floating. The steamer had broken from its moorings with nobody aware of this calamity. The entertainment continued as the craft slid sideways down the river, now five times wider than usual. The hungry pet had been on the water for most of the day, but this was the first time he had been close to any humans, meaning food wasn't far away. I don't want you to think this dog only thought about food and sleep, but, on reflection, this was pretty much it.

You might be wondering how the Rottweiler manipulated his wooden mattress over to the back of the boat. They call it dog paddle, and for a non-swimmer, he passed muster. Bump, bump, and he avoided the huge wheels, which weren't turning. The log somehow jammed at

99

the back of the vessel, and Rocky jumped aboard. The cool customer yawned, stretched, and followed his nose to the galley.

"What have we here?" said the surprised chef, knowing full well that non-gamblers were not particularly welcome on board this moribund conveyance. Being the chief cook, Sam Burns didn't take orders from anyone, and he did have a dog of his own. The grateful mutt was confronted by a large serving of Southern fried chicken, grits, and Alabama surprise, which he ignored. There was no pavlova left due to the contingent of ladies who cherished their afternoon tea.

The Showboat Queen did employ a captain and crew, but they always played golf on Sunday. The manager of the gambling hall was the one who discovered they were in mid-stream, having seen the report on the television set in his office. This is where he kept all the cash in the safe. In the cupboard, five solitary life vests awaited distribution—somewhat underwhelming considering the two hundred people currently strutting around the dilapidated decks.

"Oh my God," cried Frank Pope, which was a little incongruous, the fellow being a committed atheist. Looking out the porthole, he spied three dead cows in the water and wondered whether he should suspend operations. Management blacked out the portholes in the gaming hall because the outside world might be a distraction to punters. As he could do nothing to avert the current situation, why worry them? One of the ladies in the entertainment lounge raised the alarm.

The barbershop quartet had finished their saccharine rendition of "Sweet Adeline" when the lady in question stepped out on the deck for some air and discovered the sweeping plains underwater. She screamed.

For those who like to punt, screams are commonplace. You perform this ritual if you are female and your number comes up on the roulette wheel. So, the punters didn't stop chasing their dream. On the level above, the showroom was empty. Everybody crowded out on the deck, trying to figure out how far they were from home. The club manager wanted to maintain decorum, so he switched to recorded music without bothering to check the next tune on the playlist, the theme from *Titanic*.

Unconcerned by all this commotion, Rocky finished his dinner and looked for a comfortable spot to lie down. That log could be quite relaxing, but not so when in movement mode. His mentor favoured a waterbed, but such extravagance was not to his liking. The half-open door to the captain's quarters looked interesting, so he crept in for a reccy. In front of him, he spied a two-person divan with plush red velvet cushions. Home is where the heart is.

The helicopter alerted the gamblers, and the instructions through the loud hailer would be heard by all.

"Stay calm. A rescue mission is underway. Be prepared to abandon ship when asked."

The whirlybird departed, and Frank Pope elected himself temporary captain, declaring that gambling would continue until the liberty vessels arrived, at the same time failing to provide the government warning, identifying betting as being addictive. This is a requirement when games of chance are promoted in any form.

Yes, they did try and start the steamer, but it was useless, even with the real skipper on the phone from the fourteenth tee at Holly Hills Golf Club, way above the water level of the low-lying land. When you haven't turned over the engine in five years, a positive response would be optimistic. The only person with any technical knowledge was Blaze Lovelace from the chorus line, who claimed to have been a boilermaker in the musical *Steam Heat*.

Can you believe it took four hours to evacuate the ship? The rescue craft couldn't accommodate so many people in one go, so multiple trips needed to be organised. Controlling the transfer also proved difficult, as the rampant river threw the paddle steamer around like a rookie at a rodeo. The owners were prepared to write off their vessel and may have been glad to do so. The old darling wasn't shipshape but well insured.

Knowing what you know, can you guess which particular creature is capable of sleeping contentedly for four hours on two plush red velvet cushions? The Showboat Queen continued its journey with only one beating heart on board.

Dogs can fret when they are alone. Most of them crave company, and Rocky's inability to locate any prospective buddies disappointed him. Those who departed gathered their belongings (including the money in the safe), but Chef Sam left behind a galley full of edibles. The dog with no pals found himself fed and feeling comfortable. The sun came out, and the flow of the current slowed, until the storm arrived.

I'm not sure when a tempest is rated a typhoon, but this baby could rip the feathers off a goose. Those loose weatherboards on the foredeck disintegrated, and the craft started to creak and groan. The dog must have been giddy as the vessel bobbed like a bottle on the now turbulent waters. The paddle boat slammed into a submerged tree and was holed beneath the waterline.

Rocky's response to the continual claps of thunder was an aggressive fit of barking. However, the lightning bolts had him cowering under one of the blackjack tables before they floated away. One of the last areas to be flooded was the entertainment lounge, with the recorded music still on loop, should anyone want to hear the *Titanic* theme again.

Give the mongrel credit for deciding to forsake this form of transportation and go with something he relied on. That piece of tree trunk, still bumping along at the rear of the besieged craft, now looked dependable. The intrepid adventurer sampled some more fried chicken from the galley as the Showboat Queen started to go down. Just before this dramatic demise into the deep, Rocky slid onto the log, which remained afloat in difficult circumstances.

In the aftermath of the storm, the flooded surface changed dramatically. Uprooted trees floated on the surface, and a few cars passed by in an upside-down configuration. The destruction would be there for all to see, and later reports declared the catastrophe worse than the floods of 2011. Through it all, Rocky must have felt he was riding bareback on a buttered brumby. At any time, he may have slipped off his ride into the murky depths, but this Rotty would not give in. The dog's sense of balance impressed, as did his whine of despair, heard by a nearby liberator who thought his best mate to be nigh. Brian's version of "Ol' Man River" sounded not unlike the canine lament.

Joe Scanlan, on the roof of his house with his wife and two kids, Catherine and Matthew, first picked up on the mournful melody coming from somewhere out yonder. It took a while before he located the lost soul after young Matt alerted the adults.

"Hey, Dad, there's a dog out there, walking on water."

"Christ almighty," blurted out the shocked parent.

"No dear," said his spouse. "It's a dog."

Linda Scanlan, an English teacher, often reprimanded her husband for his poor vocabulary choices, one of the reasons he considered leaving her in the basement when he went looking for higher ground. In the end, the whole family made it to the roof, and he called the evacuation people to report the presence of a dog on a log. Hopefully, all would be well.

All did turn out well. The twin-engine runabout was well received by Rocky, and the rescuers were all rewarded with a lick on the face for their efforts. Meeting Joe Scanlan's children also proved a defining moment in this adventure. Young people understand how to communicate with pets and chose the right games to play while waiting for Ron to pick up his four-legged friend.

The waters eventually subsided, and although a hefty reconstruction bill loomed, all communities pitched in, and life returned to normal. That kennel on the verandah had been unaffected by the flood and forever became a dog sanctuary with no questions asked. Rocky never slept on a log again.

HULLABALOO

"How much is that doggie in the window?" said Kenny, seduced by the sad eyes and mournful mouth of the puppy on display. It has to be said that the dog possessed impressive acting abilities, accentuated by his desire not to spend another day in the pet shop.

"An inspired choice," replied the store owner, himself a doyen of doubtful and dubious deeds, all in the name of commercial avarice.

Kenny had recently been married. He thought love was grand. The divorce cost ten grand, and he was now looking for a partner who would be loyal and cheap to feed and didn't talk much. Little did he know the pup would grow into a beast whose appetite would know no bounds.

Baloo would have to earn his keep when he came of age, and this happened. Ken, a sergeant in the Water Police, recruited his boy to become a hull dog. When the WP vessel pulled alongside a suspect craft, the animal would jump aboard and head for the hull area, which is where most crims hide their illicit drugs. Being such a gigantic specimen, even the largest sailor didn't have the courage and strength to stop him.

How do you do? I'm Baloo.

GERRY BURKE

Few people outside this hemisphere would know the Swan River in Western Australia. Named after the black swans that frequent the region, it is at its widest when it cuts through Perth, the capital. The mouth of the water course is at Fremantle, a major port servicing international trade routes. The police have their work cut out.

With a lot of party boats in this city, the fuzz are kept busy with the trendies and their marihuana, not to mention the partygoers who go over the side without a lifejacket. The real worry is the one who, under cover of darkness, unloads an illegal consignment from a port visitor and makes a heroin run up the river. A vessel that comes to mind is the cruiser, Snow White, owned by prominent playboy Jacob Greasebum. No, he is not Jewish, but I can understand why you might think that.

The seven deckhands who work on the Snow White are not dwarfs but members of a martial arts gym. Strip back their outerwear, and you would find multiple tattoos, as well as prohibited handguns. Most of them have a criminal record, and they would not be people I would introduce to my grandmother. Jacob makes a point of never being on board during a drug run, and Sergeant Ken makes a point of giving Baloo free rein when they board the vessel.

Then there is M.V. Juliet, a former ferry. Tradition demands that all boats are female. The dog enjoys raiding this festivity of floating fun because all those aboard usually shower him with treats. The sergeant tends to be lenient with these people because they are ordinary citizens out for a good time. On a winery tour, there is likely to be drunken carousing, and the policeman likes a singalong as much as anyone.

I hope I have been able to paint a picture of the aquatic paradise you can expect in the West. There are many bridges to cross, and yachting and fishing are obvious pastimes. For homesick Italians, the gondola rides are also enjoyable.

For Kenny and his crew, their life takes public service to a new level. Cocaine and heroin usage is a major problem among the young people of this town, and those who use the waterways as a conduit for illegal deliveries are beyond contempt. This is why there is always a watch over Snow White and her crew, even when her owner is behind the wheel. Baloo had disliked Mr Greasebum since day one, and who could blame him? The fashionista only wears white suits and fancies himself as Ernst Stavro Blofeld, the super villain who likes cats. Can you believe that?

Sergeant Ken, a constant thorn in his side, will use any excuse to board the vessel with his canine companion. Captain Cocaine finds this quite irritating.

"Who gives you the right, officer, to have your people swarm over my property in this manner? This is outrageous."

"Hardly a swarm, sir. There are only two of us and the dog."

At the mention of man's best friend, Baloo produced a gut-wrenching growl, emanating from the lower depths of his bowels. Greasebum would not be happy if the animal dropped a load all over his plush white carpet.

"We are enjoying the night air on a pleasant evening. This is what you do when you own a vessel such as this. Are you going to let us continue our journey or do I have to call someone at City Hall?"

"Do that if you like, but it is three o'clock in the morning. Is there a reason you are moving upstream with your lights out?"

The two bodyguards standing behind their boss shifted uncomfortably, with their heads down. The thugs attempted to prevent Baloo from climbing aboard, but he just snapped the bargepole in two. Rehnu, the policewoman with the mutt under leash, headed downstairs to search for narcotics. This proved to be a fruitless search, as reported by sergeant to superior the next day.

Wilson Norman rated his junior officer highly and knew the tip-off came from a reliable source. Where did it go wrong?

"Both of us enjoyed a chicken dinner before we signed on. The chilli sauce may have interfered with Baloo's smelling capabilities. On the other hand, they may have been clean. We have two other vessels under surveillance—the Snow Queen and the Fairy Queen."

"You can't be serious," blurted out the police chief. "The Fairy Queen is owned by the lord mayor."

I often reflect on the people who are elected to public office in this town. The locals like them to be noteworthy individuals with a bent towards show business of some kind. Let's face it; these are the folks who gave the world Rolf Harris. The sergeant had no misgivings and would give it to the captain straight. The mayor was indeed bent.

"The bouncers detained him at the venue entrance to a Taylor Swift concert, with heroin residue found on his person."

"Bloody hell," cried Will Norman, as he reached for the phone and asked to be connected to his bridge partner, Commander Alvin Waterson.

Al Waterson had one RAN Armidale class patrol unit under his command. With a complement of twenty-one crew, the sleek and sophisticated cruising craft goes about its business, relying on its radar warning and electro-optical detection systems. The commander wouldn't need to operate the latter because his pal had told him where the targets were.

You have to be rather gung-ho to call battle stations without referring to your superiors, but this commander was all of that. Anyway, the commodore would be tied up at the Navy Club in Fremantle. Notwithstanding a nuclear scramble, lunch is always a priority.

Norman and Waterson were both anti-drug campaigners and decided to take matters into their own hands. All three suspect carriers would be destroyed in their moorings, with Baloo planting the homing devices underwater on their hulls as a target for the navy raider. The primary armament on their vessel was a Rafael Typhoon stabilised gun, mounted on the bow of the ship.

"C'mon, big boy. Let's go swimming in Matilda Bay, and then it's over to Butler Hump and Freshwater Bay. No need to wear a tie."

The downside to Baloo joining the water police was the fact that he couldn't swim. Everybody assumes woofers can dog paddle, but some are better than others. Kenny's sister-in-law, Tina, an Olympic champion in the pool, offered to help out, confident he would get down to the hull of the boat, but would he get back?

The Fairy Queen was supposed to be the first to go down, but somebody stuffed up. Baloo planted the homing device on the wrong vessel. The operators of the Dairy Queen, a feel-good antique riverboat, dispensed free ice cream to underprivileged children and were in line for a charity award. Their craft, berthed at the dock, was in line with the mayor's contemporary yacht, anchored some distance away. At the time they strafed the wooden houseboat with machine gun bullets, one hundred kids were sampling two dozen different flavours of delight. Oops!

Collateral damage is something you often hear from the military, and they get away with it because they are not elected people. The mayor tried every bit of bluster he could find but realised he would be history when the Sword of Damocles fell on him, as it would. The state premier, Denis Damocles, was on a European tour, but his doorstop comment only provided the politician with marginal support. Then, a low-life journalist let slip that the mayor owned the Fairy Queen. What if it had gone down with one hundred queens on deck?

At Freshwater Bay, Mr Greasebum scanned the horizon with some trepidation. One of his goons discovered the homing device attached to the ship's hull and dismantled it. The chap on watch saw Baloo swimming away from Jacob's pride and joy, and he raised the matter with the man behind the helm.

"These guys want to play dirty. Let's accommodate them."

As you would expect, a high-level inquiry was launched into the death of the youngsters and the part played by members of the police force and the navy. Sergeant Ken was one of the first into the witness box.

"You say that the targeting of the houseboat was an unfortunate error. Am I clear about that?"

"Yes, sir, you are. When he painted the name on the hull, the sign writer, Alan Bund, rendered the D too fancy, and it looked like an F. The dog made an honest mistake."

Baloo wasn't in the dock but by the side of his legal adviser, looking embarrassed and contrite. Body language is always an advantage in situations like this. Most people now referred to the policeman as "Killer Ken," but a measure of sympathy existed for the melancholy mastiff. The honest mistake may have contributed to the assertion of mitigating circumstance, but the fact remained that the premise for the operation was not only foolhardy and dumb but also a criminal act.

"Irrespective of your dog's unfamiliarity with the F word, are you aware that you and your buddies in the navy have taken the law into your own hands; and nominated the mayor as a drug runner?"

The man in question must have been sniffing coke all night and missed breakfast. His jacket was crumpled, his tie was askew, and he cut himself shaving. The poor guy looked a forlorn figure in the box where bravado sometimes shines through. Not this time.

"Mr Mayor, can you confirm you are the owner of the yacht Fairy Queen and use it for the transport of illicit drugs?"

Without his mayoral robes, the bounder presented as a shadow of his former self, but he stared at his accuser with the same intensity that preceded his venomous outbursts, regularly showered on his town hall acolytes.

"This is an outrageous accusation. Sure, this is my boat, but I often use it for charity functions such as the annual Pixie Festival. This blemish on my public service career is not warranted, but I am gratified that I have the complete support of the premier."

"That would be gratifying if true, but I gaze around this room and see many well-known figures. I do not see the premier."

"Yeah, well, he's in Budapest, isn't he?"

"Hungary?"

"Yes, I am, but I can wait until the meal break."

The lord mayor may not have been big on geography, but he boasted a history of winning political fights with his back to the wall. He knew the lawmen possessed no hard evidence regarding his narcotics empire and, as long as his key distributor kept a low profile, he would lose nothing more than his reputation.

Pretty Boy Dave wasn't at the inquest because he didn't like judges or juries. The multiple offender had done time, but these enforced holidays didn't deter him from the criminal activity that allowed him to live beyond his means. After obtaining work on the mayor's yacht, David the Daring managed to move up the chain of command and was now responsible for distributing crack and brown (heroin) at various nightclubs around town. The man had become obsessed with American gangster movies and always chewed gum with a toothpick in his mouth. Yes, he was attractive to the ladies but not as appealing as his associate, Baby Face Josh.

"Did you hear, Dave, how the boss went at the inquiry? Could he handle the truth?"

"If the truth came out, he would be in the clink. Right now, we've got bigger problems. Sleazebag Greasebum is trying to move into our territory. We need to butt heads."

Wow, how exciting is this? The police, the navy, and the mayor are all under the pump, Greasebum has declared war on these institutions, and Pretty Boy is gunning for the Snow White crew. It's not even the weekend yet.

Ken and Baloo were not working that weekend because they were under suspension. Will Norman had taken leave in Hawaii, and

Commander Waterson had been transferred to Hobart as the new head of the Sea Scouts. The ten-year-olds needed a leader who was strong on discipline.

The dog, still down on himself, hoped for some means of redemption. The oversized sirloin steak that his master gave him delayed his contemplations, but loyalty to the badge is paramount, and Baloo was a proud member of the constabulary. To be quite frank, any number of friendly dolphins would have been happy to plant those tracking devices, but they chose him. As it turned out, his suspension provided him with the opportunity to meet the suspected dealers on their turf.

Ken was on paid leave, but he couldn't miss the chance to indulge in a little moonlighting. Everybody does it. The public investigation put the heat on some well-known clubs around town, who didn't want the reputation of condoning drugs, although they did. Kenny and Baloo were hired for front-of-house duties, the first time a sniffer dog had been seen at one of these venues outside of a raid. Pretty Boy Dave was appalled when he arrived at Club Andree to find Turner and Hooch at the entrance. He kept walking.

Tinkerbelle, the previous door bitch, was concerned and confused. As one of the mayor's social contacts, she found the crackheads for the dealer to approach. Having been replaced by a four-legged farting machine, her work was redundant. Now, when the customers asked for some smack, they got it—across the face.

Can I say that Baloo became a target for the likes of Dirty Dave and Mr Greasebum? I can and will. The first attempt on his life happened when he departed the dog spa in Wembley. Every Wednesday, Ken enjoyed a leisurely lunch at RoyAl's burger restaurant while his companion luxuriated with a massage and pedicure on the other side of the road. The car didn't stop, with the incendiary being thrown out the back window.

As with many of my stories, the bad guys never get it right. On this occasion, the bomb exploded in a haberdashery store specialising in pre and post-natal fashion items. In the shop at the time were three children, a couple of new mothers, and a seventeen-year-old pregnant lass, still bewildered and bemused by it all. They all died, but Baloo only received minor damage to his blow wave, repaired at no extra cost by the grooming gals.

Because no one expected the target to be a dog, the culprit was thought to be a recalcitrant father or an irate clothes designer, jealous of a competitor's success. If Ken thought that, he soon changed his mind when they came at the canine with a hydraulic diesel excavator and dropped two tonnes of mud and dirt on his kennel. Fortunately, the resident had stepped out for a pee and returned to find his digs would need digging out.

Acting with admirable indignation, Kenny chased the escaping excavator and arrested the driver, the aforementioned Baby Face Josh. In doing so, he may have saved the young man from an unfortunate confrontation with the enraged beast, champing at the bit and looking for the person who devastated his domain.

While the mayor and Dirty Dave concentrated on thwarting the activities of the pavement peelers, Jacob Greasebum was ready for his retribution strike on the Royal Australian Navy. Their gunboat might not have destroyed his vessel, but this was their intention, which didn't sit well with the man in the white suit.

The luncheon for the Rear Admiral's birthday is always a highlight at the Navy Club. The officers rock up in their starched shirts and pressed uniforms, with their shiny medals reflecting off the lapping surface of their abalone soup. The miscreant was in the kitchen—a disgruntled employee who had reworked the ingredients of the oversized birthday cake to include a generous serving of ammonium nitrate. To the uninitiated, this makes it a fertiliser bomb. The organisers of the event expected to see Miss July emerge from the cake. What a blast that would have been.

The toastmaster rose to make his speech and was two minutes away from being toast, as were all the other officers in the room. The explosion took off the roof of the building and made a horrible dent in the hierarchy of the RAN. The next day, midshipman Lachlan Craigie was promoted to Admiral and asked to instigate an inquiry into the unfortunate incident. The general ranks saluted his first announcement, well received by those still breathing.

"For the foreseeable future, all lunches will be held in the dining room of the Sail and Anchor Hotel."

One doesn't like to think anybody would be pleased with such a wanton waste of humanity, but Jake Greasebum wasn't anybody. He was a diabolical fiend, maybe an ogre. Of course, these people always have a nice side, don't they?

Being a sponsor of the Pixie Festival, the charmer would invite dignitaries onto his vessel and grease their palms, which gave him access to untold opportunities. Over the years, the Pixie Festival had been a poor cousin to Sydney's Gay Mardi Gras, but this year, the parade would be on the river. The LGBTQ folks planned to lease the Rainbow Warrior from Greenpeace, and the mayor (if not in jail) would have Fairy Queen up front and centre. There is always a law and order presence, and the police intended to station themselves in the rear behind Greasebum and his numerous nubile nymphs.

"Detect one hint of illegal activity, Baloo, and I want to know about it. Do I make myself clear?"

The dog knowingly eyeballed his master and ran to the bow of the boat. Ahead of him on the penultimate craft, one of the guards with the martial arts pedigree glared back at the hound with his most menacing stare. Somehow, he didn't look so fearsome, dressed in a tutu.

The enthusiasm for the event evaporated before the booze did. They never run out of alcohol in Perth. The extraverts on each of the boats did their best to keep the party going. One of them thought it would be fun to throw the host overboard, and that's what he did, not being aware of the shark in the vicinity. These underwater creatures are renowned for having poor eyesight, but Jacob's white suit must have stood out like a beacon. With so much blood in the water, they decided to close the bar.

The police chased the predator away, and they did this with some concern for the hungry fish. The boys in blue had had a gutful of Jacob Greasebum. Now it was the shark's turn.

Somebody might also have wanted to throw the cocaine councillor overboard, but they missed the opportunity. When he returned to shore, the disreputable dude discovered a deputation waiting for him with handcuffs. Baby Face Josh had come clean, and Pretty Boy Dave shopped his boss for a deal. Where is the honour among thieves? The alderman went down for twenty years, and they held an open election to replace him at the town hall. Yesterday's villain is today's hero. I am interviewing Mayor Ken tomorrow. I hope Baloo is with him.

WILLIAM, THE WET NOSE WONDER

Kate was beside herself with grief. Well, not quite. William was seeing double. The dog tried to hurdle a soft toy on the kitchen floor and slammed into the bottom of the refrigerator. The upside to this unfortunate episode saw the inconsolable owner clasp the poor thing to her breast and whisper cajoling messages of sympathy into his ear.

A memo to all Dachshunds—you have short legs. Don't attempt levitation. It doesn't work.

William boasted other skills, and he would need them now that a junior member of the human race was vying for his owner's affections. Those bloody soft toys were scattered all over the house, and he had already been reprimanded. They were not for eating or scarifying in any way.

You can imagine the difficulty of a single mother working long hours with the Metropolitan Police. Young Harry was old enough to attend crèche, but Kate didn't like leaving the pet home alone, so he tagged along and enjoyed the playful antics of her side-kick, Andrew. Andy did tricks and mesmerised the animal with his sleight of hand, always finishing with an edible item in his fist.

When Kate and Andrew walked the beat, you would have to say that the hardened criminals of East London didn't shake in their boots. The dog with the short legs, which trailed behind, gave the gangsters every confidence they could outrun the constabulary if need be.

To his credit, the tagalong always loved the outings and made friends along the way. When the two Bobbies returned to their station for lunch, the little guy often nipped around the corner to where the Dog Squad was located. Most of these beasts were Alsatians or Rottweilers, so hooray for time well spent with others from the Fatherland. There was also a Schnauzer named Eva in residence, attached to the public relations department. Warm-hearted Willy fancied her, for sure.

Promotion doesn't come easily in the Metropolitan Police, but the pavement peelers eventually graduated to a Panda vehicle, and they put

William in the back seat. To the urchins and rogues who terrorised the neighbourhood, they were the "Old Bill" and the "Young Bill."

"Why not place the pug on the payroll?" cried the smarties.

OK, he's not a pug. Or a Corgi, if such a thought entered your mind. Small dogs are not needed by law enforcement, and this is a shame. After all, the little guy in the back helped solve more cases than Agatha Christie and Conan Doyle and deserved his legendary status.

Whitechapel has come a long way since the days of Jack the Ripper, but women walking alone after dark still need to be careful. One never knows when you will be confronted by a group of young Tories celebrating a buck's night. The patrolling Panda may be a deterrent to some, but it didn't scare the Grey brothers, who each drove a souped-up BMW with mag wheels and spoilers. Catch us if you can.

Curly and Bluey (the redhead) boasted many encounters with Kate and Andy. The sergeant and her sausage dog were often first to a crime scene, with that individual Grey odour locked away in William's whiff barometer. After a certain payroll van was done over, it didn't take the little guy long to recognise and respond to the familiar aroma of a Ralph Lauren fragrance, retailing at one hundred pounds per bottle. The driver, when interviewed, didn't say much, being terrified of reprisals, should he finger the culprits. However, his description of the two robbers was detailed and definitive. The policewoman decided against taking the matter further with the prime minister and the Archbishop of Canterbury.

The Grey brothers were tough guys, but they underestimated the technology of the day. CSI people could isolate a nose hair and place the owner of this follicle at the scene of the crime, as could William, with his superior smelling capability. At first, the hierarchy at Scotland Yard refused to let an unlicensed operative participate in line-ups, but when Kate advised that he had sworn an oath of allegiance and promised at all times to be fair and impartial, they relented.

In his first two months, the impartial one identified three rapists, one extortionist, and a bevvy of armed robbers just by barking at them. All these crims stood in front of the glass window under the number five—perhaps his favourite numeral? Those learned judges at the "Old Bailey" would not accept a dog as a witness, but an assured finger-pointer always gave Johnny Law confidence to insist number five help them with their enquiries.

There was no bigger challenge to law and order than the Grey brothers. Did I mention they were twins? Not many people realised this, with Curly being blond and the other one a redhead. This can happen when a Scotswoman moves to Sweden. The lads were bullies at school, bullies after school, and bullies on the streets. Bluey, the oldest (by two minutes), poked his bent nose and pock-marked face everywhere and scared the hell out of everyone. Neither possessed a muscular frame, but both proved menacing with a switchblade, a cosh, or a sawn-off shotgun. Curly also carried a Lugar P08 for protection.

To open a nightclub in Britain you need a club premises certificate, an alcohol license, an entertainment licence, a hot food and drink license, and insurance. Somehow, Bluey convinced the local council that he and his brother were upright citizens and would run an establishment, the envy of all. They pulled in the punters and made an effort to entice certain members of the entertainment industry to frequent the joint. Celebrities who turned up on Friday and Saturday saw comedians, dancing girls, and wannabe crooners all displaying their talents. Many of these entertainers were relatives of gangsters.

I expect you're going to ask, "Why would celebrities want to hang out in a Whitechapel club owned by hoods?" The answer is NC: nose candy. Showbiz folk consume more cocaine than anyone, and the boys provided an unlimited supply. Everybody understood this, including Scotland Yard.

The law's much-heralded raid on the premises remains memorable for all the wrong reasons. Kate and the drug squad hovered near the entrance as Andy used his magic to bypass the door bitch; Bluey saw him coming and disappeared out the back door. The rozzers swarmed while the customers were watching a show, soon to be interrupted by William, who went for the comedian. The chap tasted a bit funny, so the hungry one headed for the kitchen with more optimism. There's always something to delight the taste buds in the kitchen.

Many of those seated at tables were sniffing coke, which indicated misplaced confidence in the nightclub's security arrangements. Kate had the pleasure of arresting one of London's most controversial characters, the movie mogul Lou Strange. Lou was larger than life in more ways than one, tipping the scales at eighteen stone, but he was light on his feet. In his youth, the schmoozer had been the ballroom dancing champion at the Blackpool Winter Gardens.

In those days, you accepted the trophy and lived on your memories. Nobody expected him to become an actor and then a producer.

The fellow could recognise talent and always invested in the right productions. Being arrested for a drug offence didn't bother him at all, as his contacts would ensure he only received a mild reprimand. As Kate slipped the cuffs on his wrists, he experienced a sudden chill rippling through his body. The fragrance of her pedestrian perfume proved to be only mildly alluring, but he couldn't help but notice her fine facial features and clear blue eyes. Every man likes a girl in uniform, but this one was special—very special.

"Before you take me away, young lady, please remove one of my business cards from my pocket. Our spotters are looking for talent to support Rock Hardy in his upcoming blockbuster. Casting starts next week if you're interested."

There are many ways to entice a woman into doing something reckless and uninhibited. On top of the list is Rock Hardy. The chap, a shocking actor, had natural blond hair, great pecs, and a snug butt. The guy could have been a tight end for the New England Patriots, but he lived in old England, so he headed for the West End.

Should Kate acquire the part, she would have to ask for time off from her duties and arrange suitable babysitting volunteers for the little one. The banger would go where she went, this becoming a debatable point when they offered her the job.

"I will not accept unless you find a role for the dog."

In most cases, the casting folk would tell the chick to take a walk, but word came down from on high to hire her. So, they wrote William into the senseless saga.

Journey into Oblivion didn't have a lot going for it. The story editor managed to magnify Kate's involvement, but the script was weak, and the producers went with a first-time director, a former steward with Air Canada.

Is it cruel to suggest that the film crash-landed? Would a better budget have helped? The leading lady's performance left much to be desired, and Rock's unfortunate reputation was confirmed. One critic declared him "A shipwreck on Pebble Beach." None of the reviewers would be kind, lambasting the premise of the production, the player's performances, and the directorial debut. The only thespian to emerge with any credibility was the Dachshund.

"The dog emerged as a better actor than any of them, injecting pathos and pity into his part, as small as it might have been. One could see he would have liked to be somewhere else. My sentiments, precisely."

These kinds of comments precipitated a disaster for the effusive producer, not used to box office flops. The fellow did take heart from the positive comments regarding William's cameo, but more about that later.

One person who loved the film was Arnold Bullwinkle, a couch potato and influencer, who didn't get out much except for essential visits to McDonald's and nearby liquor outlets. General opinion rated him as a right-wing crazy, a bigot, a racist, and a misogynist. It will surprise no one that the weird whacko laid claim to over one million followers on Instagram, and his influence was not to be ignored.

The entrepreneur ought to include this guy in his will. He provided *Journey to Oblivion* with his stamp of approval, and theatres were swamped with punters, ready to enjoy the adventure of a lifetime. Mr Strange covered his costs but only just. The punters sided with the other critics and howled the film down, but there was one winner. What they did, which changed everything, was to laud the Dachshund for his performance, thus promoting him to legendary status all over social media.

So, what do you think a movie mogul would do once aware of this information? You are so right. Sign the animal to a three-picture deal. The little fella would have his own caravan on the set and receive premium dog food twice a day. Kate would act as his manager. The producer hired the best script writers and consummated a franchise arrangement, should the mongrel turn out to be as popular as expected. Hall of Fame performers, such as Mickey Mouse, Donald Duck, Lassie, and Sebastian the Crab, all generated immense appeal throughout the land, and there was no reason to think William wasn't in their class. The Dachshund was not a large presence on screen, but this didn't worry Disney's mouse.

Lou was glad he wouldn't be stuck with a duck; or crabs. Dogs can be two-dimensional, and there was a niche in the market, due to the retirement of Inspector Rex, the Austrian Alsatian television sensation. The Dachshund breeds were not new to adoration and adulation. Slinky Dog, Snickers, and others were perennial favourites for peripheral awards, and a few comic strip characters jumped out of their pages.

This was very nice, but Lou wanted his star to be top of the tree, and whatever Lou wanted, he got.

The director was impressed with William's method acting, and why wouldn't he be? Kate had taken the mutt through most of Lassie's films, and as long as they put a moustache on the bad guy, he always knew who to attack. The modern-day critic may pour scorn on this generalisation of criminal typecasting, but the fact remains that Curly Grey and his club comedian both sported moustaches.

Kate's transition from policewoman to personal management had been seamless. The head of human resources at The Met accepted her application for leave of absence, and, with the advance on William's salary, she appointed a PA, whose job was to follow her with Harry in a pram. Essentials on her shopping list included oversized yellow-framed sunglasses and designer jeans. Even Hollywood people have a uniform.

In comparison to the Rock Hardy film, this production encountered few setbacks, with the budget and time frame on target and morale high. Will was spoiled by cast and crew and lapped up the attention. One suspects he may have been disappointed his peers couldn't witness and enjoy his stellar performance, especially that Schnauzer bitch from the police compound.

Everybody looked forward to *Dog in the Bog*, filmed in Ireland and starring William, the wonder dog. A sympathetic representative of the press cited the motion picture as a "trailblazer," and Oscar murmurings remained strong. This was far from reality, with too many commercial insertions for the film to be taken seriously. Mrs Mustard's delicatessen products kept appearing at every turn in the plot. The new product launch coincided with the date of the premiere.

King William's Hot Dogs hit supermarket shelves in forty-eight counties throughout the UK, with most people recognised those floppy ears on the package. Can you imagine what this did to the royal ego? Kate dragged Big Ears along to the BBC and ITV for talk show appearances with Graham Norton, Jonathan Ross and Chatty Man Alan Carr. There he was, preening himself in the company of Elton John, Michael Caine, and Dame Judith Dench, with the reviews yet to be published. They were positive, and everyone breathed a sigh of relief.

🐾

Three months after the release of William's second movie, the little digger, Kate, and young Harry moved into their five-million-pound residence in Wapping. Those hot dogs just walked off the shelves, and the mutt and his mistress were heading for Easy Street.

Don't ever let it be said that the latest newcomers to high society would forget their roots in another part of East London. Even with his new-found fame and fortune, William was still an inquisitive dog, and he loved those roots. His mistress remembered those days and nights on the beat when her boy would forage his way around Stepney, Tower Hill, and Bethnal Green, digging up whatever he could find. These scavenger hunts were often productive: he unearthed three mobile phones, Mr Finch's false teeth, and, on one occasion, a twenty-pound note.

Some folks might snigger at this change of luck and question why they needed such an enormous house. Well, the PA moved in to supervise Harry, and another girl was required to service the dog's Twitter account. Let's face it. This star of the silver screen was no one-hit-wonder. *The Case of the Drowned Sardine* smashed box office records from Hammersmith to Hoboken in New Jersey.

When you've got it all, sometimes you can forget how it all started, although the animal could hardly fail to recall those desperate days sniffing bins outside fast food eateries. Now, William was a regular on the social pages of *The Barking Gazette*, a popular journal produced by the Dagenham Vet Clinic.

One thing missing in the dog's life was romance. These things can happen. Movie-making is not a nine-to-five job, and opportunities to mate are rare. Blame the hero of the moment for this situation, as he didn't want any competition on the set to divert attention away from the star. This didn't mean there weren't bitches hovering around the stage door, waiting for Bill the Bull to present himself. Kate soon nipped that opportunity in the bud. Every evening, she and her associates were collected in a stretch limo and transported to their hotel.

Now, let's talk about heartbreak. Sergeant Eva, the Schnauzer, was the object of Will's desire, no doubt about it. Eva appreciated the attention but, for all her false modesty, didn't see this cowboy as a suitable match. The fact is snooty Schnauzers look down on Dachshunds, and that's the way of etiquette and equality in the canine world. William and his willie would have to explore other options.

The trip to Canada was an initiative of the public relations people, always keen to expand horizons.

"The numbers don't lie. Our guy has many fans in Quebec and Montreal; resident Francophiles regard him as a typical French dog. Some personal appearances will cement his popularity."

There would be no argument from Kate, who had never been to these places, and Harry was wild about maple syrup. A friend had also returned to his job with Air Canada and offered advice. The lady baulked at some of his proposals.

"Kayaking at Niagara Falls is not on our bucket list, Julian, but if you have some more genteel suggestions, we would be interested."

William was against the trip from the start. After taking one peek at the Husky on the cover of his travel voucher, the coward scurried off to his kennel.

Canada! They have bears there.

The new international idol and his entourage arrived in Montreal to be met by Prime Minister Bublé, who professed to be a fan. Give us a break. Michael's children were the fans, and Kate made sure they each received a photograph of the superstar, appropriately paw-signed.

In terms of personal appearances, the PR people mapped out a wide-reaching excursion tour, incorporating London and Windsor in Ontario, Churchill in Manitoba, and Prince Edward Island on the east coast. The team would also travel to Labrador City, where the dog struggled with an image problem.

Those market research studies are so important, aren't they? Did you know that Bill Clinton and Vladimir Putin both own Labradors, and Margot Kidder (Lois Lane) spent her younger days in Labrador City? None of this related to William's lack of popularity in this remote northern outpost. The folks just didn't like sissy dogs. The place was cold as a mother-in-law's kiss, but William, always on alert for bears, didn't complain. Kate arranged a photo shoot with some Mounties, to curry favour with the locals, and they all pressed the flesh at the only cinema in town. An Indian family, on holiday from Delhi, provided the guest of honour with the adulation he was used to, but that was it. The dejected dog carried on like a trooper, as one does. Hopefully, the situation would be better when they arrived in Calgary for the Stampede.

The Calgary Stampede is the biggest and longest-running rodeo in the world, and this significant tourist attraction draws over a million attendees. Our four-legged friends are fascinated by the chuckwagon races because it's a dog-eat-dog competition with no quarter given or asked for. Should any of the chuck fall from the wagon, this is when the fittest and fastest earn their stripes.

William didn't have to worry about anything like that. At the Hyatt Regency, the little guy was looked after very well, with Kate being a generous tipper. The exciting news from the seventh floor was the guest in Room 715. Kathy Carmichael from Kamloops, BC, had moved in with her peripatetic poodle, Penelope. These two cowgirls would go anywhere for a chuckwagon event and wouldn't miss this weekend for the world. Kathy, the manager of Rebecca's Roughriders, had moulded her girls into one of the finest teams in the land. Penelope was their lucky charm and a more charming bit of fluff you would never hope to meet. The yellow and orange bob on her backside gave her added appeal.

The two women met at breakfast. The pampered pet was taking his tucker in the suite; otherwise, the prissy poodle may have been pursued around the premises by a persistent predator, intent on having his way with the angelic creature.

"Not ordering the flapjacks, Katie? Is there something wrong with our Canadian food?"

"Not at all," replied the fussy eater. "I'm British. We take tea and toast for brekky, but young Harry likes his maple syrup. He could live in this part of the world."

Kathy accepted this explanation as she palmed off a piece of pancake to the ever-alert pet beneath the table. Before the conversation drifted into banalities, it became obvious that the women had something in common; Kate was a former policewoman and Kathy a serving member of the Canadian Mounted Police. Her chuckwagon activities were something of a hobby, and she always took her leave in Calgary in July. With her butch haircut and "Popeye" tattoo, she presented as one hard-headed woman, although the gal must have lost some credibility with a poodle trailing behind her.

"When you head to Stampede Park, today, I should warn you to guard your pet. A lot of Inuit come down from the Territories and the Yukon. Their meal of choice is Arctic fox, but they have been known to barbecue a sausage dog now and then. Penny is also at risk, as are other small animals."

"Goodness gracious," exclaimed Kate. "Surely they wouldn't skewer a screen star. They must have seen *Dog in the Bog.*"

"I doubt if Lassie made it to their part of the world," suggested the Mountie with conviction. "Some of those igloos have bad TV reception."

Thank God William didn't hear this conversation, because his star was about to wane. After one day of focus, the fickle public turned their attention to the rodeo and associated activities. To make matters worse, the organisers bumped him off the official guest list in favour of Justin Bieber. Can you believe that?

With no promotional duties to be undertaken, Kate offered to mind Penny while Kathy revved up Rebecca's Roughriders before their race. This would be an opportunity for Will to wag his tail and meet the sassy senorita with the colourful ass. Harry would be happy watching American soap operas at the hotel with the PA.

Having two dogs on leads in a crowd is no walk in the park. With the little critters so close to the ground, they may get in the way of the Boot Scooters, off to take in the Shania Twain concert. Then it started to rain. The slippery saddles made it challenging to ride those broncos, and the chuckwagons slipped and slid on the muddy waters. Nevertheless, the Roughriders overcame these obstacles and won their event. Kathy had nothing but pride in her heart. William had an ankle in his mouth. One of those Boot Scooters had kicked Penelope in the midsection, but she was fortunate to have a hero at her disposal. If you've ever experienced an angry dog attached to your leg, you know they are not easy to dislodge. The aggression persisted until the bug-eyed and bloodied Canuck fled the scene, full of regret and disbelief.

The heavens opened up, chaos reigned, and people ran for cover. This was indeed a stampede. Kate had nothing but her Stetson cowboy hat to protect her hairdo, and the yappers panicked. So much so that Penny slipped her lead, before being swept away in the deluge running down the embankment towards Elbow River, which meandered around the park.

"We are celebrities," yelled the embattled Brit. "Get us out of here."

No one was listening, so she gathered her charge in her arms and headed back to their hotel as quickly as possible. The centre of town was within walking distance, and a bath and a hot toddy waited for them. Harry continued to binge-watch his American soapie, but the news wasn't good about Penelope. The poor thing had been squashed to death during the stampede, and Kathy was distressed, as you would expect.

"The Lord giveth and the Lord taketh," said the eloquent vicar as he blessed the small coffin, which contained the remains of the peripatetic poodle. Kathy chose to bury her friend at the dog cemetery on the edge of the prairie, and her peers turned up on their horses to provide comfort and solace. One of the Mounties arrived with his Husky pup to inject some canine respect to the service, but William chased the little fella off.

Kate felt a certain degree of responsibility for the outcome, as the misfortune happened while the sweet thing was under her care. Kathy would have none of it and wished them well as the visitors prepared to return to "Old Blighty." Lou Strange had been on the phone. The contract for a new project was ready to be signed.

Did I mention the sticking points with the new contract? James Bond wanted precedence in the credits. How ridiculous. Just because he shared the same name as MI6's finest didn't mean he was a leading light. There was also pressure from Mrs Mustard's company, once again bankrolling the production. King William's Kosher Cocktails could be a sensitive product if one planned to release in Casablanca. The fact remained—the dashing Dachshund wasn't Jewish.

These problems would resolve themselves as time went by. In the interim, the iconic actor would have to whip himself into shape. All those pancakes in Canada had taken their toll, and William appeared a little heavy on the ground. The manager, on the other hand, looked good. All she seemed to consume was tea and toast. Incidentally, the protest in the chuckwagon race was not upheld. Rebecca's Roughriders did not interfere with the wheels of their competitor before the start. At least, that's what the judge (from British Columbia) decreed.

The police reunion was important to Kate, to be held at her favoured Tooley Street pub. William also liked to spend time in the Kings Arms, it being a dog-friendly ale house. There aren't many of them these days. Perhaps a certain Schnauzer from you know where might turn up? Some of the retired officers brought along their pets, and a fine time was had by all. William's celebrity status became a talking point, and he was happy to paw print the photographs, which were always produced on request. Fame can sometimes be as fickle as fun in Finland, so it is always best to embrace every moment you have, at least until your wheel of fortune is disabled.

This is what those at Frogmore Pictures hoped would happen. Anticipating a strong demand for the next children's movie, they signed Felicity Frog to an exclusive contract. Felicity, the daughter of Kermit and Miss Piggy, was proud, pugnacious, and pinky green—a star in the making. The owner of this company once worked for Lou Strange, but personality issues damaged the relationship. London's beastly tabloid *Animal Antics* broke the story and didn't hold back.

"Dog v Frog" screamed the headline, which pleased the publicity people. Free advertising is priceless in situations like this.

With the prospect of formidable competition at the box office, the studio trainers put William on a treadmill and reassessed his diet. Miss Piggy had found the transition from television to the silver screen difficult, but Felicity was a stunner, so the dog from the bog would have his work cut out. To fast track his production, Lou gave Mr Bond a better credit and promised to release in Tel Aviv. There would also be a gala tour to the colonies beyond Canada (less rain in Australia), and a Royal Garden Party was on the cards.

This would be a coup for William. With so many princes and princesses in attendance, they would never invite a frog.

ATTICUS

Naughty, haughty, almost forty! He was the Duke of Finchley. Sir Gregory, as his butler called him, impressed as an imposing figure, but he proved an embarrassment to his immediate family because of the spicy scandals that kept recurring. The media couldn't get enough of him.

Gregory didn't leave out his loved ones when he moved into outrage overdrive. They suffered like everyone else, and, at one stage, even his dog disowned him. Atticus was on a good wicket: two square meals a day, grooming, games with the servants, and access to forest walks, where the deer became his friend. One of those dear friends provided him with refuge when the hound left home.

The separation didn't last long. A Hungarian Vizsla, as with most dogs, has this inherent loyalty to their master or mistress, irrespective of their standing in the community. Need I mention that even serial killers have pets? The return of the prodigal son proved to be a low-key event. He slid under the gate and padded around to the back entrance of the castle, where the dog flap remained well-oiled and welcoming. Without making any fuss, he made his way to his kennel in the alcove and settled down for a well-earned kip. Further down the hall, two knights in shining armour looked on approvingly. OK, there weren't any knights in the armour, but it was nice to have everybody's pal back where he belonged.

Gregory was having dinner when the reconciliation took place, and genuine joy emanated from everyone involved in providing the master with his meal. Whispers went back to the kitchen, and the maids passed on the news to the housekeeping staff—Atticus is back. Hooray for the joyful occasion, better appreciated because the duke was sober.

Not many people would have been interested in Finchley prior to the exploits of their favourite son. Today, the district is a well-populated residential suburb, but in medieval times the region was verdant woodland, surrounding villages whose inhabitants supplied pigs and wine on the vine to London. The grapevine also included stories of scandalous gossip and outrageous behaviour, mostly leaked by the duke's personal staff in exchange for a silver penny.

This story takes place somewhere between the two time periods mentioned above. To save embarrassment, I will not name the monarch involved, but I can say the duke occupied twenty-seventh position in the line of succession and sat comfortably on the perimeter of any royal censure. Should something like the Black Death come along and dispose of those with more potent claims, powerbrokers in the palace might be prepared to take more interest.

"The man is almost forty years of age. He ought to be married."

This came from a widowed neighbour with a spare spinster in her household. The frumpish Lorelei Lee spent too much time knitting; otherwise, she would have made an excellent wife for someone but not a playboy. The duke preferred buxom babes who liked to party, and there were plenty of willing participants in that neck of the woods. With the castle surrounded by woods, opportunities existed for outrageous Bacchanalian orgies. Or have I been watching too many *Midsomer Murder* episodes?

In his capacity as a faithful friend, Atticus attended these festivities and helped clean up the mess in the form of leftover food. The energetic playmaker enjoyed the Roman toga parties the best. When the frolicking folks removed their footwear, he used to steal one sandal from someone and swap it with another. Can you understand what it is with dogs and shoes? They sure are besotted. One can only think of Venus, the frequent companion of Imelda Marcos, who is purported to have owned three thousand pairs of shoes, which must have been bliss for the little tyke.

If there's going to be a heel in this story, it's not going to be Atticus. Yes, playful, but he didn't have a malicious thought in his head (that anyone knew about). The dog loved everybody, and everyone loved him, especially the servants. Every year at Christmas they made sure he received a large bone wrapped in a yellow ribbon. Gregory always shared his eggnog with him. A lot of people assumed the duke to be rich beyond comprehension, but this was not true. The peasants who paid rent on his landholdings were not wealthy, with the pickings slim. He did receive income from a business source in Nottingham. Robin Goode ran a redistribution organisation, whatever that is, and shekels found their way south every month.

The king of the castle owned Finchley F.C., a legendary sporting institution that recruited members and participants from the surrounding district. I don't know who came up with the idea of kicking a pumpkin around the village green, but it caught on. Atticus, as team mascot, offered encouragement and motivation, when the players were down on form. He would seek them out during the break and nuzzle them aggressively; the team knew they would have to lift their game. The mutt also delivered the half-time fruit to one and all. The orange dog was everywhere.

Above everything else, the peripatetic pointer embraced the hunt, which always happened on a Sunday, with Gregory leading the charge in his red jacket. With many hounds involved, they wouldn't stop yapping, but most of them accepted Atticus as boss, so proceedings progressed smoothly, except when they didn't.

Scout possessed big ears and a big mouth and was owned by the Earl of Middlesex, whose extramarital encounters were on the high end of shameless, but that's another story. His dog, an egomaniac, didn't like being bossed by the cur from the castle. So, a mutual feeling of dislike existed. At the first summer meet, when the pack went after the foxes, the two dogs went after each other with teeth bared. A nasty business! They eventually returned to the stables, wounded and bedraggled, to receive a severe reprimand from their owners, witnessed by a member of the fourth estate, on hand to report on the event.

Public figures are always under scrutiny, and several scribes delighted in providing titillating gossip on page three of the four-page notice board in the village square. If the villagers didn't like the story or its implications, they would pelt the news facility with eggs and tomatoes. This is how they discovered omelettes.

The duke's affair with Goodwoman Molly Peck didn't make the notice boards, but the town crier knew about it. However, there was no way he would enrage the Lord of the Manor and spend five days in the stocks. The lady had every right to visit the residence for vegetable deliveries on a Friday, but she really wasn't a good woman and always lingered longer for mead, molasses, and other sweet treats.

Are we talking about mead as an aphrodisiac? Maybe, although both parties were naturally uninhibited, and the end of the week is always an appropriate time to let your hair down. Atticus stayed in his kennel during these trysts, and the armoured guards in the hall always had their visors closed.

A more controversial incident would be the deflowering of the delectable Dinah, the darling of Dorking, more recently "Queen of the May." Just sixteen years of age, she looked forward to receiving

129

her crown from the visiting dignitary. The kid was excited. At the reception, she met Sir Jeffrey, Sir Andrew, Sir Donald, and a whole heap of freeloaders. Any one of them might help her with her desire to become an actress. Why wouldn't she accept a mug of strange-tasting mead from the guest of honour?

That was Saturday. The young girl arrived home on Tuesday to announce she would forgo her studies to sign on with an acting class in the west end of Finchley, the same drama school that gave the world Judi Wench. Reluctantly, they let her go, only to see their daughter return some months later, barefoot and pregnant.

After reading these stories, some people may think the duke was some kind of a cad. Not his faithful friend in the alcove, who thought his master could do no wrong. There may have been a bit of jealousy if those women stayed too long, but they never did.

The best times were the one-on-one pheasant shooting expeditions. This is what Atticus was bred for, and he loved the outings. Sometimes, Gregory shot a peasant by mistake, but that can happen. There would always be reparation of some sort, which indicated a level of care and sympathy not often appreciated by others.

One thing that soured all these cherished moments was the advent of the Black Death, which cut a swathe through most of London and many towns and villages. The aristocracy was affected to the extent that Sir Greg avoided anyone or anything sporting black spots, including the Duchess of Dunberry and her Dalmatians. I could go on about the duchess, but I am aware minors will be reading this absorbing tale. No one is more beholden to family values than yours truly.

Changing the course of history requires an earth-shattering event, and this bubonic plague gave historians something to write about. For a start, twenty-six people in the line of succession all perished, which made the Duke of Finchley heir apparent; Atticus was on the way to becoming top dog. Can you believe that?

Standing in his way stood the monarch's Great Dane, Louie, an introductory gift from the French ambassador. Surprisingly, the mastiff cross was a bit of a sook and spent too much time with the ladies at court. The dopey Dane should have been sent back to Copenhagen for retraining.

Louie

Was it palace pressure or his sense of responsibility that forced Gregory to change his ways? The fellow stopped drinking and became more circumspect with members of the opposite sex. Now that he looked like being next in line to be crowned, many folks wanted to throw their arms around him. As the plague still lingered, he discouraged such familiarity and remained at Fortress Finchley, happy with his dog for company and visiting vegetable merchants.

Molly Peck and her husband survived the pandemic because they ate their own fruit and vegetables, as did Sir Gregory, who often praised Molly's melons. When life returned to normal, those close to power considered the inevitability of the duke's ascension to the throne. To give his credentials more authenticity, they discussed the possibility of anointing him Prince of Wales. This didn't go over well with the current titleholder, Thomas Jones, a strong voice for his people in the House of Lords, as were Burton, Bassey and Hopkins in the Commons.

It was not unusual for the supreme ruler to hand out titles as a reward, and those who sat in the upper house did so by right of birth or royal decree—not the case in the House of Commons. One had to be elected. Neither should family succession be regarded as an automatic

131

fast track to the throne. If Lord Muck possessed a bigger army than you, you would more than likely be heading for the Tower of London. Most people are familiar with the War of the Roses.

Sir Gregory boasted an attractive rose garden, but he didn't have any soldiers, which made him vulnerable. In this instance, competition would come from the north. Bonny Prince Jimmy, a Scottish firebrand, suffered from delusions of grandeur and always had his eyes on the prize. Should he hijack Gregory's tilt at the top job and become the supreme ruler of Great Britain, everybody would be having porridge for breakfast. This wasn't the worst part. The highlander spoke with such a broad accent that no one understood a word he said.

The Scot harboured no love for the Sassenachs, and the duke and his woofer seemed easy prey. Like many people, the cocky jock underestimated the orange dog.

It would be Robin Goode from Nottingham who sent the warning to look for Scottish soldiers heading south. Being a true friend, he diverted five of his best archers to Finchley to provide support. Gregory despatched Atticus to the village green to recruit the footballers, even though the plague reduced their numbers. He also granted sanctuary for the villagers, as he expected the marauders to show no mercy to those in their path. The Scots would pass through Sheffield Wednesday and arrive Friday. Should they be worried that it would be Friday the 13th? Attacking a castle sounds easier than it is. One contends with solid fortifications and that boiling oil that comes down from on high is quite inconvenient. The Finchley fortress also included a moat which, on this occasion, would be confrontational. Attenborough's Alligator Farm was an animal conservation initiative, but the critters might be leased out should the price be right. Gregory, the sweet talker, pounced.

One should also mention another type of animal with access to the pet flap that opened onto the drawbridge. Due to the accuracy of the Nottingham archers, Prince Jimmy and his force were forced to retreat, which allowed the drawbridge to be lowered and the dog let loose. In a ten-minute foray, Atticus managed to kneecap or ankle bite fifteen foot soldiers before he bounded back home to comfort and safety.

The footballers threw pumpkins, provided by Mr and Mrs Peck, but the hard-shell peas proved more effective. Used in a slingshot, they could be directed at the heads of the swarming invaders. Some of the poor buggers, who were hit in the eye, staggered about and then fell into the moat to be at the mercy of the alligators.

In the end, Jimmy and his fellow rebels fled the field of combat and repaired to bonny Scotland to enjoy a humble Hogmanay. Gregory and his band emerged as national heroes. In recognition of the support given by Robin Goode, the lord of the manor paid for a statue of an archer to be built in the town square. This is one of two monuments that survive in Finchley, today. The other one depicts a naked lady and is far more popular.

Rumour has it that the woman is Molly Peck, but I cannot confirm this conjecture and wouldn't want to. Reports indicate that her friend did promise her the position of Minister of Agriculture once he ascended the throne, still a long way off. In Wales, opportunity was fast overtaking convention. The person previously known as Prince had died, with the title ready to be appropriated. Thomas Jones' widow Delilah made a half-hearted attempt to claim it for herself, but women's rights were still hundreds of years away.

So, they invested Gregory and confirmed him as the king in waiting. This didn't go over well in the West, but one doesn't like to offend Crown officials, who have control of the purse strings. In an effort to salvage some pride from the situation they found themselves in, the burghers gifted a litter of Welsh Corgis to the titleholder. This didn't go over well with Atticus.

What do you do with a bunch of puppies? Sniff them out? Feed them to the alligators? With no young people to supervise petting sessions and the like, the fighting dog worked hard to amuse them. What a come-down! Only a matter of weeks after he carved his name in glory, he was a nursemaid.

"Hey, Atta-boy, how's the new family?"

Gregory, who noticed his pal was not coping, took the opportunity to take the mickey. He received a deep-seated growl in response as the canine crept away to his kennel for some me time. The future ruler, as part of his orientation activities, was required to spend some evenings at Hampton Court, breaking bread with the main man and his entourage. Why not take Atticus along to give him a break? The monarch welcomed the beast, thinking his boy would bond with the Hungarian hound. What a miscalculation!

The dog fight in the middle of the dining hall proved to be a battle royal. At first, the odds-makers refrained from taking bets, but once they observed the ruler and his guest committed to the contest, they opened their satchels and plied their trade. The big boofhead opened the betting as early favourite, but as mentioned before, he was a bit of a sook and ran away from the encounter after being gouged by Atticus, the fearsome fighter from Finchley. Gregory couldn't have been prouder and happy to relieve the king of some of his sovereigns.

With the heir apparent spending more time with the first family, the next in line concluded that an absolute ruler should indeed be married. This point of view had been whispered in his ear for some time, and now, with his fortieth birthday almost upon him, he realised that it might be time to settle down. Most people would not be shocked by his decision, although his choice of spouse came from left field.

Do you remember that frumpish spinster with the knitting needles—Lorelei Lee, his neighbour? Over the years, she knitted a few cardigans for the duke and, in recent times, helped out with walking the dog. So, the lady was not so frumpish anymore. And talk about cheeky! She called him Lord Cardigan (not to be confused with the gentleman at the Charge of the Light Brigade) and Prince Pullover and generally scoffed at the pomposity of his official duties. He liked that, and he liked her.

They married on his birthday, with Atticus being part of the wedding party. Guess who didn't go on the honeymoon to Margate and sulked in his kennel for five days?

What about me?

The newlyweds enjoyed their time in Margate, a town with circus acts on the foreshore, wandering minstrels in the streets, and some hot moves from the Morris dancers. Back in Finchley, chaos reigned, with the Corgis running amok and getting under everybody's feet. The scullery maid dropped a priceless piece of porcelain and was mortified. Peck and Peck Aviaries, whose owners were cousins of Molly's husband, sold a red robin and a finch in a cage to the chief housekeeper, who hoped this diversion would amuse the puppies. The finch had a fine musical voice, but he wouldn't let up.

"He rocks in the treetops all day long
Hoppin' and a-boppin' and singing his song.
All the little birds on Jaybird Street
Love to hear the robin go tweet, tweet, tweet
Rockin' Robin"

Atticus had half a mind to kill a rockin' bird and would have done so if the alligators had still been in the moat. Fortunately for the feathered friend, the snappers were now reunited with Yeoman Attenborough. This would be the start of a frustrating time for the ambitious dog. As most Brits would know, the heir apparent sometimes has a long wait before transition takes place. In this case, the incumbent lived until he was one hundred and two years of age. At least Atticus outlived the Great Dane, who expired with a whine and a whimper. What a wuss!

I feel sorry that the hero of this story never achieved the status he craved, to be the royal male he always wanted to be. Everybody's friend was delivered to God some ten years after the brave defence of his master's realm and was honoured with a plot in the castle grounds. All of the Corgis turned up for the funeral and paid their respects. The dour defender of democracy had become their mentor, albeit a mentor whose bark was worse than his bite. Tell that to Prince Jimmy and the Caledonians.

CORGI AND BESS

Bess had been a royalist since the day, as a child, she waved a small flag in the coronation procession along Whitehall and Pall Mall. She had been named Elizabeth, after the elegant and charming heir apparent, who would go on to become the longest-reigning British monarch ever. Yes, her mother was also a monarchist. Her dad wanted to call her Bobby, after a famous footballer.

Throughout the years, the Queen became a role model for the loyal woman. If the ruler appeared at a function wearing white gloves, you can bet Bess would soon have that fashion statement high on her list of priorities. Of course, she couldn't afford to buy them at Harrods, but Debenhams produced an acceptable alternative. Princess Elizabeth's marriage to Philip was a grand affair and more or less confirmed the legitimacy of marrying a sailor. Bess's young man was only a leading seaman, and all his hands were not on deck. Shore leave gave room for talk of commitment, but there's always bad luck around every corner. The lad drowned in a boating accident at Henley.

Was this the trauma that affected all her future romances? It might have been, but on reflection, I can't recall many other romances. I was a recent arrival at the time, finding my way around London town. Not having much money, I didn't go clubbing, so I joined the local library, where Bess held the position of chief librarian. We often discussed the books I read, and I valued her advice. Without it, I would still be reading penny dreadfuls.

In time we bonded, and I considered her to be my agony aunt. I recognised a liberated woman but a lonely one. Thinking I had the answer to the problem, I gave her a dog for her 30th birthday. There was not much thought involved in deciding which breed I should acquire. Charles, the Pembroke Corgi, could have been any one of the Queen's brood, with a reputation for being loyal but suspicious of strangers. You guessed it. He was Welsh.

Charlie was the light in the librarian's life, and her siblings noticed the difference as their sister became more sociable and fun to be around. Dominic, Richard, and Harry were all married with families but always supported Bess. I was occasionally invited to one of their homes and knew them as Dom, Dick, and Harry. The latter gentleman could be a loose cannon, but he always produced a tasty fluffy duck from his well-stocked bar.

Prior to the reign of Henry VIII, Bess's family were all Roman Catholics, but along came the reformation, and Henry started hanging these people by their toes. Today, the woman and her four-legged friend are staunch members of the High Church of England. Every Sunday, they trundle into London and find a pew at the back of Westminster Abbey. Should a Welsh choir be singing the hymns, Charles would sneak down the aisle to obtain a better view.

The day the dog attacked the Archbishop of Canterbury was an occasion of severe embarrassment, and if it wasn't for my commitment to the truth, I would hesitate to document it. The great man, adept at glad-handing parishioners after the service, didn't spot the animal until too late. There was no physical attack, but man's best friend wouldn't stop growling and barking and continually circled the holy man as he tried to evade the disgruntled dog. The problem appeared to be his red robes. Certain animals are afraid of this vibrant colour, and I can confirm this situation, as I have been attacked several times in my red tracksuit. Bess gathered up her pet, apologised to the reverend, and departed for home, where she gave Charles an orange. He didn't mind orange.

On reflection, the archbishop was not the only one to observe aggressive behaviour from this small beast. When the ticket collector on the Baker Street bus tried to collect a fare from Madam, the mongrel nearly took off his hand and could have been evicted. Of course, the woofer was right. The lady couldn't find a seat, so why should she have to pay? These days, they don't have conductors, so now and again you'll see a Pit Bull going to Paddington.

Bess did have one complicated romance, which I am reticent to reflect on because he was an older man who worked for the government; if you must know, I'm talking about MI6. I can't remember the year, but I do recall a bitter winter, and they stayed in a lot. She would buy the wine and he would arrive with a pizza pie, the pie that came in from the cold.

Because the fellow came from Cardiff, you would think he and Charles would hit it off but not at all. The dog saw the interloper as a wedge between himself and her ladyship. Neither did the visitor ever share any of the pie with the hungry animal. Bess tried to mend the relationship but to no avail. One day, the man of mystery disappeared, and an iron curtain seemed to have been drawn across her social life. Rejecting further overtures from men, she applied to join the Communist Party, as did the Corgi. Both would fight for the depressed, distressed, repressed, and downtrodden and work enthusiastically to acquire equal rights for women. Emily Pankhurst would have loved to have somebody like Bess in her corner, advocating one of her militant entreaties—Trust in God; she will provide. The almighty has come a long way since 1903. Just ask the Vicar of Dibley. We now have female clergy, heads of state who wear a dress, and non-binary people. Can someone please request God to stop what she is doing? Where will this end?

The owner of the library didn't like the librarian bringing her politics into her workplace and was especially critical of the small hammer and sickle flag on her desk. The writings of Karl Marx and Friedrich Engels were filed under "Enlightenment." Her comrades often dropped by with pamphlets and details of forthcoming meetings. They always brought along a treat for the dog.

Considering that Charles didn't like the colour red, you would have to think he would not be comfortable in Red Square, a destination target for his mistress. She had been chosen as part of a cultural exchange delegation, but getting a place for her companion proved difficult. Bess argued strenuously with the travel director.

"You can't leave a paid-up comrade behind. He won't cost you anything. The dog can sleep under the bed."

Peter Anthony was a clever facilitator and a long-term party member who maintained excellent relations with the Russian Embassy and Aeroflot, the carrier of choice for the delegation. The travellers would have preferred British Airways, but the prices were poles apart, and BA's daily flights now ended in Warsaw because of political instability.

"OK," said the pragmatic planner. "Let's put him in the cockpit with the pilots but no special meals. The dog will eat borscht and blini like everybody else."

Memories remain from this ground-breaking trip but few photographs. This is why the picture of the travellers outside the Kremlin is so definitive. The dude with the four short legs was the only one in the group not to be considered a possible spy. The Russians are paranoid, and with good reason. Spying brings its rewards. If you can hoodwink Boris and the other Pasternaks, there's a book deal in the offing.

Did the KGB know about Bess and her friend from MI6? If so, she wouldn't be walking Gorky Park for long. Charles must have reckoned this bit of turf to be a better alternative than Red Square, as he discovered dogs of the opposite sex on the snow-covered paths. There also appeared an apparatchik who always walked his black Labrador just before lunch. Not many officials in Lubyanka Prison enjoy a meal break, so Vladimir Putin must have been important.

"Hello, major. Nice dog. Do you speak English?"

"I do, but the dog doesn't. Are you from England, da?"

Bess was impressed that the man with the military bearing was able to identify her accent so quickly. On the other hand, he could have been following her on purpose, which would be cause for alarm. With a microfilm embedded in the dog's collar, she wouldn't want to see Charles arrested. Her dearly beloved assured her that there would be little chance either of them would be apprehended. Can you really trust a British spy?

I have no intention of telling you who in the Kremlin hierarchy provided the secret intelligence, but the information involved a spy in the upper echelons of MI6. There had always been suspicions of a mole, but he must have acquired plastic surgery. All of the bigwigs boasted sharp jaws like Dick Tracy and sharp minds. Uncovering the traitor would not be easy. Getting the microfilm back to the UK would not be easy. Bess had declared that she was up for it.

"I am with the cultural arm of the British Communist Party, here to share views and promote artistic values."

"Ahhh," said Putin knowingly. "My division employs cultural attachés in many embassies around the world, and they understand nothing of art. You are indeed a prize of the Soviet Union."

The KGB man gave her a wink and wheeled off after his dog, which had found something of interest and was going his own way. Bess wondered if her discomfort had been detected. At twenty degrees below zero, one shouldn't be sweating like a pig. And what about his bravado? The temperature was freezing cold, and the man with the great pecs was just wearing a T-shirt.

Back at her lodgings, Elizabeth appreciated the warmth of her bed chamber and thought about the man she met in Gorky Park. Was he just a winker, jailer, soldier or spy? Her room would be bugged as a matter of course because these people suspected everyone of everything, but what if Major Putin turned up again before she completed her mission? The woman had been chosen for this assignment because she had no previous contact with anyone in the intelligence community before her recruitment in the library. If the Russkies were onto her lover, they might be onto her.

That night, Bess joined the others in the dining room, counting the hours until she would be aboard the return flight home. Team leader Maggie Boyd cast her eye over the menu.

"Oh look, they have Pelmeni and Ponchiki. What a treat!"

Charles, the dishlicker, found the kitchen, where the staff spoiled him rotten. Not being a fussy eater, it didn't matter that none of this food would ever be seen at Sainsbury's. Nobody knew they were feeding a Moscow mule with a critical state secret around his neck. The Cold War could be wonderful at times.

Bess, halfway through her Chocolate Salami, nearly gagged when Vladimir Putin entered the room, accompanied by a senior officer dripping in medals. The lady felt a lump in her throat, and it wasn't anything she had eaten. The waiters fussed over the new arrivals, so one would think they were top brass. Eyes down and concentrate on your dessert. Thank God Maggie had something to say.

"We've acquired tickets for the Bolshoi, which are hard to come by; all down to your friend, Bess—Major Putin."

"What?" exclaimed the stunned delegate. "I know nothing of this. The gentleman in question is over there, but I have only met him once."

"You must have made an instant impression," stipulated the envious bachelorette, a dance tragic, delighted to be going to the ballet.

On their way out, the suspicious senorita decided to be proactive and dropped by the other table to thank her new friend for the theatre tickets. The Labrador owner introduced her to his superior, and she wondered how he knew her name. No doubt, those at the front desk of the hotel had been helpful.

"We look forward to seeing you during the intermission," said the sly soldier in a voice redolent of fragrant anticipation. Librarians arc not a species susceptible to flattery, and Bess guessed this man could attract any number of beautiful escorts should he so desire. She would have to be on her toes, but for the moment, she would relax and watch others on their toes. The Bolshoi was world class.

For a bunch of East End commies, drinking Champagne at the ballet was not something they would likely report on, but they did have an excuse. The buggers didn't stock Newcastle Brown Ale. This was not the kind of proletarian lifestyle they expected to find in Moscow, and some maintained their rage. All of them mellowed when the military men joined the party, both smoking like a chimney.

"The Soviet Union is proud of our artists, male and female," said General Babkin, eliciting a positive grunt from his companion from the KGB. "Soon, our troupe will be able to tour internationally, once we overcome these squabbles we are having with the West."

"Gosh," said Maggie Boyd. "This would be a large travelling company. The Bolshoi has over 200 dancers."

"With 200 support staff from the Kremlin," added Vlad, the inhaler, glad to be the font of all wisdom.

When Bess returned from her night out, she realised her room had been done over. Small items had been moved and not replaced. I have a cleaning lady like that. With Charlie in the room, it might have been different, but if the hotel advertised a dog-minding facility, why not use it?

The head of this facility didn't report to the KGB, so Charles was not under the same amount of scrutiny as his mistress. He was, however, under scrutiny from the other pooches in the compound, which meant a continuous struggle for respect. When the struggle turned to violence, the collar around the Corgi's neck became scratched and scruffy, with the microfilm torn and tattered. Bess was appalled to see the damage when she arrived to pick up her charge, just as Major Putin came through the door and suggested a nightcap.

How would she keep him away from the animal? The bellboy came to the rescue.

"You would like dog in your room, which I can deliver, da?"

"Thank you, Sergei. Very kind of you." It was also kind of her to slip him one hundred roubles for his trouble.

"Your companion, General Babkin, he is not joining us for drinks?" asked the now composed woman, ready to defend her virtue by any means possible.

"Sadly not," replied the major, who was much more assertive in his own company. "The general does not drink vodka in public, although he is an enthusiastic consumer in private." This comment came with the whisper of a smile, which surprised Bess. Vladimir Putin was not a humorous person.

The man seemed disappointed his guest decided on a non-alcoholic beverage, but she needed all her wits about her. Perhaps he didn't desire her body after all. The information he provided shocked, which is what he intended.

"During the performance of *The Dance of the Sugar Plum Fairies*, a member of your delegation made a sexual advance on one of our officials. Homosexuality is forbidden in the Soviet Union."

"My goodness," said Bess. "Surely not Nigel. Did your official reciprocate?"

It would be Putin's turn to be shocked by the candour of the Englishwoman. His reply sounded less strident than his earlier comment.

"Let's not talk about that. Homosexuality is forbidden in this country."

Bess knew her travel partner to be promiscuous, but he had been warned to behave himself while in Moscow. One had to be worried for his safety.

"My friend, I hope, will be given the appropriate legal advice should the matter end up in court."

"Don't worry. There are many lawyers in Lubyanka. In the meantime, I must offer you my goodbyes. I have been transferred to Leningrad, where I shall make my mark. Can I wish you and your dog much pleasure for your remaining time in our country?"

With that, the mysterious major retreated into the night, and Bess ordered some vodka. The experience wasn't as bad as she thought it might be. Perhaps if the gentleman made his mark, he might be a handy contact if she ever returned to Russia. However, right then, one needed to think about poor Charles. Left alone in their room, he might be tearing up the place.

Not so. The mutt was fast asleep on her bed, obviously exhausted. Settling down beside him, she turned out the light. In the morning, the dog collar received running repairs. The film was not too damaged, and Bess slipped it back between the stitching. After using her nail polish to repaint the leather, everything old was new again. Of course, questions needed to be answered, particularly about the scrutiny they were under. Was this normal practice, or had the mission been compromised?

It was not unexpected that the visitors would be manipulated by state-sponsored guides at every public event, so MI6 arranged the handover of the microfilm in a clandestine manner, attached to a fact sheet handed to Bess as the group entered St. Basil's Cathedral. What an imposing example of iconic architecture! The dazzling display of paintings and wall art proved too riveting for anyone to notice the woman slip the piece of celluloid into her pocket. Most people would be familiar with the colourful onion domes and painted turrets which give this sixteenth century monument its place on the world heritage list. The cathedral is eleven churches in one, and now a museum and tourist attraction. Commissioned by Ivan the Terrible, the temple of magnificence was nearly demolished by Stalin the Terrible. Those prickly punters from Peckham and Putney walked the walls, completely gobsmacked.

So much for the first day of activities; now, the delegates had been parted. Maggie fronted the welcome desk at Lubyanka Prison, trying to obtain Nigel's release, and Bess received permission to attend a dog show. Charles, never having seen a Siberian husky before, absorbed every word his mistress quoted from yet another fact sheet.

"The breed is from the Spitz genetic family, so they must be able to swim and are intelligent, friendly, and outgoing. Just like you, Charles, although I doubt you can pull a sled."

She could have mentioned that he was good in bed because this precocious pet made sleeping an art form. On this day, the little fella was alert, excited, and probably wondering why he couldn't be involved in the contest, being well-groomed, faithful, sometimes compliant, and handsome to boot. Was he getting the eye from that attractive Husky over yonder?

Bess enjoyed the show but was mindful of someone giving her the eye, not that he wished to be observed. Anyone wearing a trench coat and an Ushanka fur hat is sure to be state security, so Charles would have to be on his best behaviour. The microfilm would be there for the taking if someone chose to carefully examine the band around his neck.

The rest of the culture vultures were taking in the Red Army Band, performing without their orchestra and dancers. The Alexandrov Ensemble is the official choir of the armed services, and they are so patriotic you want to throw your finest glassware into the fireplace. Shortly after this performance, the deputy team leader was informed that their return flight had been brought forward to that afternoon. Three of the original group were not notified of this change in arrangements, and Lindsay Dove didn't care. He wanted to get home for the football match at White Hart Lane.

This is how Maggie, Bess, and the dog were left behind to fend for themselves. Nigel was still in consultation with his lawyers.

Over the next five days, they tried to spring their pal from prison, and Maggie attempted to book them a seat on a flight to anywhere. No such luck! The support from the arts council withered and died on the vine, and the bureaucracy proved to be endless. Someone didn't want them to leave Russia. Someone thought one of them had something to hide, but they didn't know where to look.

At the hotel, expenses started to escalate, including their bar tab. One night during happy hour, the desperate house prisoners were swimming in their vodkas and listening to the incessant balalaika music over the PA system. All of a sudden, Carole King's version of "You've Got a Friend," drifted into the room, and the two women looked up in anticipation.

Who should arrive but Sergei, the bellboy, carrying an envelope, which he deposited on their table?

"Evening, ladies. Bernard Blight from Blackpool. I hope this letter is everything you hoped for."

Then he was gone. At least to the foyer to respond to the constant call on his services. Maggie pounced on the envelope before Bess could react and read the message out loud.

"We'll do what we can
For three poor souls
Wait for our transit van
At 1 a.m. she rolls."

"Who the hell is we?" demanded Maggie, having lost trust in anybody from the country she once admired and venerated. Bess wondered how to explain without further comprising herself.

"I do have a friend, who is vain, untrustworthy, unreliable, belligerent, and usually drunk, but I can't help loving that man, the one who is charting our getaway from this difficult confinement."

Before any more enquires could be made, she rose from the table and headed for the elevator with the team leader in hot pursuit. It was Sergei who pressed the button for them and confirmed the arrangements.

"Meet me at the fire escape on your floor at 1 a.m. Please keep the dog quiet."

"What about Nigel?" questioned Maggie. "We can't leave him behind."

"Your friend will be in the van," said the young man from Blackpool as the lift ground to a halt and the doors opened. "Soon, you will all be gone with the wind."

It is unlikely the lad had ever read Margaret Mitchell's novel of the Deep South, but he may have seen the film on video. Pirate copies were available throughout Moscow, as the censor caused havoc with mainstream movies. At one stage, Dr Zhivago was banned.

At the appointed time, two women and a dog presented at the top of the stairs and followed the bellboy to the lane below, where a white van with blacked-out windows awaited. After a quick reunion with Nigel, everybody jumped aboard, and the vehicle slowly headed out of town. Why attract attention by breaking the road rules? Forty minutes into the trip and the Corgi was asleep on the floor of the transport, with the passengers ready to ask the driver where they were going.

"We're heading for Smolensk, Minsk and the border, where we hope to sneak you into Lithuania. Help is already waiting in Vilnius."

Unfortunately, the KGB was waiting in Smolensk. Nigel had been released from jail by his gay friend, a bureaucrat at Lubyanka. The remaining delegates were found to be missing from the hotel, and agencies across the country were put on alert. All of this was anticipated by MI6, who ran operatives in most provincial cities. Bogdan Bogdanovich, alias Bert Fluck, would flag down the van just short of their first destination and continue transporting the passengers in his Lada sedan. They would have to dress like peasants, and he brought along suitable clothing. When Charles woke up and discovered his social standing had deteriorated, he barked his disapproval.

Only a true local knew the back roads of this town, but Bogdan once lived in Fulham, so he was a quick learner. He intended to reconnect with the people carrier on the road to Minsk, but before then, he drove the famished souls to his residence, where his wife fed them. The good woman even produced a bone for the dog, the most important passenger, although not everyone was aware of this.

In Minsk, the KGB employed sniffer dogs who knew what English people smelled like—something to do with their diet. Fortunately, Charles knew what Rottweilers smelled like and barked like hell when they were in the vicinity. Some might think Rotties can be put off their game with a loose flung bratwurst or two, but it ain't necessarily so. Those who have sworn the oath of allegiance are particularly vigilant and would like nothing better than to forgo a bite of sausage for a bit of Pembroke Corgi.

Would the crossing into Lithuania be a bridge too far? Bess and Maggie now cradled Uzi machine guns in their arms. That's how serious world politics had become. Khrushchev was banging his shoe at the United Nations General Assembly, and the British security services plodded about in disarray, disabled by treachery and treason. Could they repatriate the little dog home and benefit from the secret he transported around his neck?

"Charlie is hungry," said Nigel, perched on a rocky outcrop, surveying the road ahead. Bess was practising her quick load on the Uzi, while Maggie preened her eyebrows. They had been transformed from peasants into a unique fighting unit, unique because none of them had ever fired the guns they carried. Safe harbour beckoned, but the last miles are always the hardest.

"Charlie is always hungry," suggested his owner, ready for sustenance herself. "Perhaps we shouldn't move until dark."

The getaway vehicle, having done its job, was now on the road back to Moscow. With the border only half a mile north by northwest, it could be seen that the lookout towers were few and far between. With no further radio contact available, they were on their own. Nevertheless, MI6 operatives kept tabs on where the fugitives had been dropped off and were close by. The girls dreamed of a hot bath.

In the moonlight, the countryside looked deserted, but they dared not use the torches provided by Bogdan.

"Gee, it's only a high wire fence and a strip of dirt," said Nigel, who was quick to arrive at the final obstacle. Ladies first, I think, as he gave Bess a lift onto the structure.

"Not without my dog," came the reply, and Charles found himself sitting on her neck with his arms around her throat. This was getting more degrading by the minute.

The sturdy wire proved easy to grip, and Maggie was right behind Bess, with you know who in the rear, which wouldn't have surprised anyone. The surprise was the arrival of the Russian armoured vehicle and the soldiers who spilled out with their machine pistols. I read about a situation similar to this in a book, with the escapees cut down mercilessly.

This didn't happen. Nigel turned out to be the Audie Murphy of the Second World War. The gunslinger sprayed them with bullets from his Uzi and then tossed a grenade into their midst. What a guy!

The secret service saviours finally arrived on the other side of the fence to repatriate the girls. The agents threw a blanket over the razor wire, and the enthusiastic females jumped into their arms, something the gay deceiver also enjoyed, and he wallowed in the congratulations he received from one and all.

The reunion between Bess and her man was not so joyful. She let him have the dog collar in the face and stormed off for her hot bath. The Corgi, recalling his dislike for the chap, did the only thing he could think of. He peed all over his shoes.

THE COLLIE CALLED WALLY

Wally was a star, according to his boss, Molly. It was unusual for a sheep herder to be female, but the young girl was the son her father never had. Her mother was around in the early days, but didn't like the wide open spaces and ran off with a corset salesman from Condobolin.

The McKenzie property was a little north of West Wyalong and not on the tourist track. Father and daughter only owned a few hundred woolly wonders, so Wally coped. The Border Collie—keen, tenacious, energetic and athletic—would run about on the backs of the sheep and have them doing cartwheels. Molly just whistled.

Some folks questioned this type of life for a teenage girl. There was no problem with her schooling, but the young bucks who came around were rude, crude, dim-witted dudes. Michael McKenzie wanted more for his daughter, so he sent her to an agricultural college, where she met more dim-witted dudes. I didn't meet Lance Boyle, but I imagined the worst.

"G'day, babe. How are they hangin'? Did you enjoy the cool lecture on artificial insemination? It had me all horny."

Lance, the prick who made everyone sick, terrorised all the girls in her class, but Molly derailed his most ardent overtures.

"I'm not your babe and never will be. Dangle your dick somewhere else."

The fact that the four-legged flitabout expected to graduate at the same school made things easier for his mistress. With a growling dog beside you, you can be as cheeky as you like.

My visits to the campus were only fleeting, as I studied journalism elsewhere, but my cousin was one of the lecturers on the back of his beastly endeavours in another place. How he understood so much about artificial insemination, I'll never know. Molly and I got on well because I knew people in Back Creek, not far from the McKenzie farm.

The final year of the girl's degree course must have been tough. The floods took their toll, and bushfires were the norm during summer. To make matters worse, Mick struggled with gout, and his daughter got pregnant. The good news was that Lance Boyle was not the father of the child. Neither was I.

Gout is a painful and restrictive condition. So is pregnancy. Both adults attempted to maintain their herding activities from atop the corral fence, and this worked. With the mongrel around, the bleating blighters knew who was boss. The collie even managed to take a mob to the sale yards unsupervised.

Molly gave birth in the hospital at Parkes with her dog by her side. He didn't deliver the baby, but most people thought he could have. The furry friend vetted the visitors, primarily there to check the DNA.

The baby was named Carol because it had been a Christmas affair—not that anyone admitted paternity. Having done his sums, Michael concluded that he couldn't blame anybody at the college because the dalliance must have happened during the holiday period. Perhaps his daughter had colluded with a dim-witted dirtbag from Derriwong or Daroobalgie. These towns were known to be devoid of eligible women, and the menfolk boasted ferocious reputations, except for the ladies' hairdresser.

Being a single mum doesn't worry the girls of today, with the stigma of past generations relegated to the rust bucket of reality. It didn't take the breadwinner long to get back in the saddle, with Dad as the child-minder. Ignoring his gout, he was giving his granddaughter instructions on how to drive the tractor. What a family!

Then came the tragedy. With his reduced mobility, Michael considered other ways to be useful, with gardening fast becoming an obsession. The enthusiast planted flower beds all around the house with Carol as a willing helper. One day, he stepped on a rake, and when the handle smacked him in the head, he dropped to the ground unconscious. Assistance arrived, and Molly helped load the poor fellow into the ambulance, but one of the paramedics, unfamiliar with this particular carrier, didn't latch the back door correctly. The ambo struck a bump at Devil's Crossing, the doors flew open, and the stretcher was ejected from the mercy vehicle.

Michael didn't know what hit him, but I can tell you—a forty-tonne timber jinker, ten wheels and all. So much for the hospital delivery. The driver drove straight to the morgue. They pushed his remains under the door, then off to the garage to fix the lock. The girls were devastated, and the accident became the lead story in the local press. I heard about it from my cousin at the ag college, although I'm sure he didn't subscribe to the *Trundle Times*. He might have had a closer link to the girl than I thought.

Bad memories linger longer than you think, so Molly decided to sell the farm and all her stock. With Carol and Wally, she moved in with Aunt Dolly, a dietician in Deniliquin. The lady had once been a dancer, but she didn't like talking about those years. Now, with a steady job, she leased a three-bedroom weatherboard in an elegant part of town. Her daughter was the same age as her niece.

"Polly, put the kettle on. We've got visitors."

"Hello, Dolly," said Molly. "It's so nice to see you back where you belong."

This was certainly a reference to those dancing years, but I'm not going to go there. The hero of this story is the dog. Wally always received an agreeable reception from the relatives, but this time they were going to stay, which might test the relationship. The household was formerly a cat-friendly environment, but Felix electrocuted himself on the Christmas lights after over imbibing in Yuletide milk. Dolly decided not to replace the irreplaceable.

"My goodness, how the child has grown, and look at the hound from the pound. How ya doing, big boy?"

The boy in question jumped all over the happy housewife, and not just because of the goodies in her apron pocket. He enjoyed renewing acquaintances with people he liked, and it was great to leave those sheep behind. Some of them had real hygiene problems.

I may not have mentioned it, but the Border Collie was a rescue dog with no previous sheepherding experience. Mick McKenzie found him at the pound and took pity on the poor wretch, who had been mistreated to the extent that a kick up the backside was his nightly due whenever his previous master returned home from the pub. Michael always said the Collie maintained pent-up aggression from these episodes and took it out on the jumbucks.

The newcomers embraced the change of lifestyle and liked living in a large town. Well, a large town compared to what they were used to. Denny was a magnet for those who lived in the Riverina region, one of the biggest areas for Merinos in the country. In fact, in 1861, the first stud was established there by English migrants. Nicole Kidman's cardigans are all Merino wool. Enough said.

When Molly landed in town, the current cultural event was the reality TV program called *This is Your Wife*. Trying to find a partner for single farmers was the gist of the show, which was shameless and embarrassing, with the girls showing more ink (tattoos) than the blokes. They filmed before a live audience in Deniliquin, so the young lady from the sticks needed to be involved. She rocked up with Wally at her heels, but they wouldn't let her friend in. He departed, annoyed and irritated, but not for long.

The herder's notorious nose picked up a familiar aroma, and off he went, heading for the sale yards. Cattle and sheep trading is important for the economy of this town. Once inside the perimeter fence, he rushed around like a headless chicken. The owner of the premises, Willy Woolnough, not happy with his junkyard dog, noticed the show-off performing his antics. The foreman was tasked with investigating his credentials.

"Whose sheepdog is that? I like his form, and he's not intimidated by the rams."

So Willy gave Wally a job. After a period of grace, the stockman came to an arrangement with Molly to lease his services. It wasn't nine-to-five employment, but trading days came around quite often, so this was a nice little earner for the new girl in town.

As time went by, local folks bonded with the sentinel of the sale yard. On auction mornings, he made his way to the facility and put in a hard day's work. Returning to his kennel, he would enjoy a quick kip before taking on Carol in a game of "Fetch the Fat Football." Well, more of a stuffed sock than a football, but they both relished the challenge. One day, the youngster presented, but there was no dog.

"Where's Wally?" cried the lass, highly agitated. Her mother tried to placate her.

"Don't worry, sweetheart. He's probably doing some overtime. There are lots of sheep to round up. You remember sheep, don't you, buttercup?"

By morning, there was cause for concern. The dog's breakfast remained untouched, and, as the pooch never missed brekky, questions were asked around town. Had anyone seen the mutt?

The consensus was that he had run off with one of his girlfriends, who might have returned home with an empty transport. This was close to the truth. The bitch's name was Barbara, who had committed to a stock consignment destined for Canberra, the nation's capital—by rail. The denizen of Denny hopped aboard the freight carriage just before the wheels started rolling and stared out the door in despair as the train gathered speed. Let's not discuss what might have gone down in that carriage between Deniliquin and Canberra, but the two dogs travelled quite comfortably compared to the other passengers. They don't have first and second class in live animal shipments, just eighth class. The bitch had a job to do, but she was on downtime until the consignment arrived at its destination.

The endpoint of this delivery is irrelevant. Barbara and Wally parted company when she was required to supervise another stock transfer. He could have assisted, but when you are a stranger in town, you like to get a feel for the place.

The doorman at Parliament House was surprised by the appearance of the dog, which came out of nowhere.

"G'day, mate. Who do you belong to?"

The sniff test of the doorman proved fleeting because he had nothing of value for the hungry hound. Several people were arriving for the morning's parliamentary session, and the Liberal member for Barker appeared to be a more promising target. Angus Cowper, the pride of South Australia, maintained his seat for many years, irrespective of which party was in power. The silver-tongued devil currently held the position of minister for foreign affairs and was indeed a player—Magda, Yvette, Gerda, Natasha, whoever. At home, he was a devoted family man, with his petting restricted to two dogs and a cat. Certainly, an easy touch.

"Hello, fella. Where did you come from?"

The screening guards were not happy when the MP waved aside their objections and escorted the canine into his domain. His people flocked around the new arrival and almost killed him with kindness. An urgent order went out to the Queen's Terrace Café for nourishment, and he then slept it off in a corner of the minister's office.

Parliament House is a maze, but Wally enjoyed the adventure. If he spied any security staff coming at him, he would dart off through some door or another and in so doing, he initiated friendships with the prime minister, the chief whip and the cleaning ladies. They often shared opinions prior to high-powered talks with the Chinese ambassador or a state premier.

When the Japanese came to visit, the DFAT (Department of Foreign Affairs and Trade) dog welcomed the VIPs at the banquet by mimicking the heads down/heads up greeting of the Nippon officials. What he didn't know was that he would be part of the exchange of gifts, which is customary for these types of functions. Wally would be heading to Japan. Crikey!

Decisions such as this require considerable research. Those tasked with determining what might be a suitable gift for a visiting prime minister discovered the chap loved the movie *Red Dog*, about a kelpie in Western Australia. The idiots at DFAT didn't understand the difference between sheep and cattle dogs, but the fact that he could nod his head made it a slam dunk.

"Do you think he will like Japanese food?"

"Who cares? He is here and handy. Let's fast track his visa."

Japan is on everybody's bucket list. I go there frequently due to their persistence in putting on a classic horse race every November. However, what are the odds I would run into Wally in Tokyo at a sumo wrestling match?

I had only met the animal on a couple of occasions, but I suppose he remembered me because of my distinctive odour. Dogs can smell fear in anyone. He was all over my face with more licks than you would find at an ice cream tasting. The sumo thing was down to his companion, the PM's chauffeur, who had been given the job of walking Wally every day. The young man insisted on passing the auditorium and often bet some of his hard-earned on his favourite wrestler.

The chap looked at me with suspicion and refused to accept my request to take my friend out for sushi. With the dog back on the leash, I could do nothing about it but made a note to ring Molly when I returned to Oz. One seems to recall a reward on offer for any useful information concerning the missing pet, probably not payable in yen.

Can anyone forget the prime minister's re-election campaign, with his popular pal a definite asset? Their whistle-stop rallies are no different to ours, and Wally was the warm-up act. Japanese people had never heard the whining chorus from "I'm the Sheik of Scrubby Creek," and it cut through all the white noise that dominates such events. The dog joined forces with a prominent rap artist, and they released a local version of the song.

Isn't it amazing how Australian culture permeates the most resistant regimes?

Chad Morgan—"The Sheik of Scrubby Creek"
https://www.youtube.com/watch?v=DWfFFMcfEt4

THE DOBERMAN DIDN'T LIKE DOUGHNUTS

Obviously, he was not a police dog. With a reputation for being a brave guardian and noble companion, this export from Deutschland is regarded as a cut above the rest.

If you own a Rottweiler or a German Shepherd, you understand these animals will be vicious, vengeful, and vindictive. They never got over the fact that their country lost the war. Adolf Hitler owned Alsatians, while most of the Gestapo favoured Rottweilers (Hermann Goering kept lions). The mayor of Frankfurt, a pacifist, made do with a sausage dog.

The aforementioned information is of no significance to this story. It is just some of the useless data swilling around in my head, waiting to break out.

Dogs don't frown. They prick their ears. Discerning human sounds can sometimes be difficult, and the poor dears find it challenging to tell the difference between screaming and singing. When the lads arrived in their hot rods, screaming rubber, this proved too much for Mac. The Doberman Pinscher lived with his owners at the end of a dead-end street. Beyond this point lay a bituminised plot of land that once operated as an aerodrome landing strip. This is where the petrol heads came to show off their wheels and practise their doughnuts. If you thought this tale might be about something else, you were mistaken. This dog would eat anything.

Animals have this innate ability to form relationships with anybody. Even politicians have pets. With no possibility of getting any sleep, the inquisitive one decided to venture over to the source of the syncopation and see if he might be able to negotiate an arrangement. Those of you who have ever tried to negotiate with a Doberman will know they don't often hang around to consider your point of view.

In this instance, the black beast took three steps and sailed through the open window of the souped-up Mustang. Danny Finley, with his

155

buzz-cut hairdo, took fright and bolted out through the driver's door, leaving the dog to reflect on his options. Mac had never driven a vehicle before and this one headed towards the council tip at speed. You would not be surprised if I told you the vicious vigilante arrived home smelling like a pig in a puddle of pong.

Chronicle a day in the life of this pet, and you would find our champion always busy, being an enthusiastic gardener with exceptional bone-burying skills. He would chase birds all day if you asked him to, and what can one say about his shadow dancing? Although his humans were often engrossed in their financial affairs, he loved them to bits and considered those afternoons on the back verandah discussing free market economics as gold. Sure, he didn't contribute much to the conversation, but Kathy and Andrew liked the fact that the pooch seemed to agree with everything they said. The canine kept nodding his head.

Mac's magic moments gave him intense satisfaction, but never let it be said that his mentors didn't harbour memories of their own, like the day the relief postman tried to deliver a package via the side gate. Mac was under the house at the time, chasing a snake. When the new man entered forbidden territory, the dog realised he didn't smell right and went for his ankle. Ouch!

Johnny Feehan thought he knew it all, having delivered mail in this neighbourhood for ten years (but not on this route). The usual guy rarely took ill, but, in this instance, JF stepped into the breach and did so with too much arrogance and overconfidence. At the Post Office, there existed a list detailing those properties that might conceal a savage creature. Surely, it would have only taken a minute or two to prepare himself for the possibility of a "Mac attack?"

The mongrel maintained a firm grip on his ankle, and the pain was excruciating. The postman tried to kick the aggressive beast off but to no avail. At the third attempt, the Doberman released his hold but came again, this time locking-on to the bottom of the man's trousers. The tug and pull continued until, in an act of desperation, the postie undid his belt and slipped out of his pants. The poor guy was seen running down the street with the dog in hot pursuit. Witnesses to this hilarious episode reported seeing the terrified fellow wearing his wife's knickers.

This last comment was not true. The regular postman returned to his route and confided to Kathy and Andrew that Johnny wasn't married.

Which brings me to the unbelievable tale of Matt Griffin's utility.

Matt used his vehicle to transport his chooks from the farm to Chicken Magic, a popular franchise in the city. Bruce Halligan, a low-life petty criminal, appropriated the ute as his getaway car after he robbed the bank in the same location. Matthew had this habit of leaving the keys in the ignition as he unloaded his cargo.

Because he possessed hero potential, Mac could sniff out a bad man from three blocks away; Bruce, on the loose, fitted the mould. The whiff of pre-cooked chicken might also have attracted his attention. When the Griffin utility cartwheeled into Lavender Avenue, the dog was sitting on the driveway, alert and ready for anything. The stolen utility stopped at the end of the road with nowhere to go, so the bored animal hurdled the front fence and jumped aboard the fleeing conveyance as it turned around and departed the unescapable escape route.

Being distracted, the driver didn't spot his passenger in the back. He had spilled out his ill-gotten gains on the seat beside him and noted a haul of cash amounting to about eight-hundred dollars; also, a promissory note from Rupert Murdoch and a medium-size brown paper package, possibly full of bearer cheques.

No such luck. The parcel was the teller's lunch, but handy if you have to eat and run.

When the fleeing thief discovered a dog staring at him through the back window of the cabin, he wasn't fussed, until the brute bared its teeth.

The Victoria Police look at theft as a serious matter. Only minutes after the robbery, they alerted their air wing; the spy-in-the-sky departed its helicopter base, looking for a battered utility reeking of frightened chicken. About to arrive at the Paris end of Queen's Road, Bruce considered two alternative choices of direction: Princess Avenue or Duke Drive, the panoramic boulevard of magnificent views (if you exclude the abattoirs). The crazed criminal decided on Princess Avenue, but he misjudged the ramp and sent the vehicle through the railing and nose-first into the river. Yes, you guessed it. The crim couldn't swim, nor the hundred dollar notes, which fluttered out through the window and settled on the calm but wet surface of Melbourne's pre-eminent waterway. With arms flaying about in a desperate attempt to float, the chap was visibly distressed, but who on dry land would put their life on the line to save a small-time robber? No one that I know.

Although not recognised as an Olympic event, dog paddle shouldn't be underrated. The canine headed for the drowning motorist, grabbed his collar in his teeth and dragged the lucky fellow to safety, where he was set upon by account holders of the National Bank. The arrival of the police helicopter saved the scoundrel from further bodily harm, but they arrested him and carted the fellow off to the remand centre.

Kathy and Andrew arrived at the scene and discovered their pal would probably receive a commendation for his efforts. At the very least, he would be in line for a Neighbourhood Watch award. People who didn't like the dog said he was nosy.

Sure, he used to sit in the driveway every morning and observe the world go by, not that there was much to see in a dead-end street. Sometimes, he latched on to a passing pedestrian and went wherever that would take him. On most days he found his way home in time for breakfast. Of his preferred companions, you couldn't go past the statuesque jogger and newsreader, Naomi. The news-hungry hound never missed the evening bulletin, curled up at the feet of Kathy, who was always interested in the financial report. He didn't like Channel 7, as one of the reporters irritated him, which left Naomi on the ABC. On air, she projected as the personification of no-nonsense journalism, but in her designer tracksuit and Zoom Pegasus running shoes, she was a feather in the wind. Mac followed her everywhere.

A few days after she reported on the robbery/river fiasco, they found themselves together again, heading for the same location.

"No," said the beautiful broadcaster, "Let's try Duke Drive today. We don't want any busy bodies around."

At that time of morning, no one ventured down Duke Drive. This route was indeed a picturesque alternative, but it didn't go anywhere. Nevertheless, there were many adventures available for a dog off the leash. Distracted by an aroma, the slack bodyguard discovered himself quite a distance away from his escort and didn't see Ricardo, the rapist from Richmond, hiding behind a sycamore tree.

OK, just because the chap was covered in tattoos doesn't mean he came from Richmond. However, he wore a football jersey and looked pretty nasty. If Naomi had seen him coming, she might have put those sports shoes into top gear, but the brute jumped her from behind. Fortunately, the reporter was in good voice, and her ear-piercing screams punctured the tranquillity of the morning. Mac made a beeline towards his lady friend and recognised the footy jumper as something to sink his teeth into. He came at the thug with aggression not witnessed since Tiger's last victory at the PGA championships. The ugly incident featured on the ABC news, with Naomi reporting on her own near-rape experience. She is currently favourite to win her first Walkley Award.

The dog moved on, as you do, but suffered the media attention afforded those who dabble in heroics. As a famous figure, he now attracted invitations from many organisations and went on a barking tour to raise money for animal rights, often performing from the rear tray of a Mack truck.

Was it wrong for Kathy and Andrew to benefit from their guy's fame, be it ever so fleeting? You could order a mug shot with a paw autograph for less than five dollars, and Mac Snacks were every dog's dream between meals. The autographed poo bag also proved to be a best seller.

In time, everything settled down, and normal service resumed. One couldn't fail to notice the Mercedes now in the driveway, but there was still room for Maciato to maintain his morning ritual, now sitting on a sequinned mat, recently purchased from Taj Mahal Floor Coverings, a much-admired retail outlet nearby. The piece of carpet wasn't waterproof, but neither was the dog. If it rained, he would stay in his kennel.

🐾

Politics can be a frustrating business. By the time you become used to your local representative, the other mob wins the election on the back of outrageous promises.

"Get out of here!" screamed Andrew. "They're going to move the council tip to next door."

Those four little words were not false promises. Two "For Sale" signs appeared on the street within days. Somebody scheduled protest meetings, and the kids down the road dumped rotten tomatoes on the minister's front lawn.

The idea was to dig up the old aerodrome area and put the landfill underground. A chimney would be built for the dissipation of the supplementary stench. Kathy commented that their dog produced wind, but this would be something else. The minister for the environment deflected pertinent questions at the protest meeting.

"Nike Air is building a factory outlet on the ground floor. Would they do such a thing if a pollution problem existed?"

"Then why are they staffing it with robots from Japan?" came the retort from a local nerd who worked for an artificial intelligence company.

The minister tried to reply but was drowned out by booing and hissing. Not anticipating the rotten tomatoes coming his way, he fled the scene. Not only did the government rogue rush through the permit process, but he insisted that groundworks start at once. The haulage trucks lumbered up and down the one-way street all day, and two more "For Sale" signs went up. The sentinel at number nine was not impressed.

"Andrew, we can't leave Mac outside in the dust. He'll end up with a lung infection."

Sometimes, Kathy made sense. Their last vet bill was a little short of the national debt, which is why one needs to avoid a medico with a mortgage. You should hear what he charges for a sex change operation.

So, they brought their pal inside, and with his head on Kathy's lap, he listened to the discussion concerning the future. Let's face it; with the value of their house spiralling downwards, selling didn't appear to be a great option. Questions need to be asked, and the little woman had plenty.

"Do we know what the odour will be like?"

"Burnt cat, I would imagine," said Andrew, shrugging his shoulders.

At the mention of the word "cat," the dormant Doberman raised his head and scanned the surroundings. Confident they were still alone, he relaxed and committed himself to the ongoing exchange.

"Thank God the refuse will only be vegetable matter, which might smell like soup."

"We should be so lucky. By the way, are the Campbells still coming around to play cards tonight?"

"To my knowledge, they are. Best we lock Mac in the spare room?"

The dog didn't like the Campbells, who owned a car similar to the one that did doughnuts on the bitumen. Call it "wheelies" if you like, but the Doberman was distressed by this type of behaviour, and you don't want a distressed Doberman in your house, believe me.

In my profession, I have a lot of trouble getting people to believe me. Some folks don't accept exaggeration as an art form, but most people understand having a tip in your backyard is the pits. Alright, technically, it wouldn't be in their backyard but close enough. Then there is the prospect of living with robots as neighbours. What would they talk about?

The trucks continued to roll through Lavender Avenue, and the weeks rolled into months. The big hole got bigger, and the occupants at number nine looked on in awe. At least they were not ignored by the contractors, conscious of the inconvenience this truck traffic caused. The foreman always dropped by when something awkward might happen, and the residents considered him not a bad sort of chap. Can you believe his name was Charlie Hoberman? No, I didn't think so.

When Hoberman met the Doberman, it was love at first sight. This guy wasn't born yesterday, and confronting irate residents with vicious pets was nothing new to the dude in the hazmat jacket. That's why he always carried a pork chop in his pocket.

"How do you do, Mr Maciato? Have you eaten?"

With the hungry animal out back ferociously feeding himself, Charlie provided an update on the construction program.

"Our work will be done when we finish extending your road to the facility. However, you don't have to worry. This access is only for Nike. The tip trucks will enter via the old entrance down the way. How do you feel about that?"

"Well, I don't know," said Andrew. "I suppose Nike Air is cleaner than last week's leftovers, although my sweaty gym shoes don't have a lot going for them."

That's where Charlie left it. More would be disclosed later. The sports shoe manufacturer indicated they would donate a pair of trainers for everyone in the street, who would also receive a fifty-page document explaining the configuration of the state-of-the-art recycling plant to be built. So, it wasn't going to be landfill. I suspect most of my readers would be unfamiliar with the mechanics of a commercial regenerating operation. I certainly hope so.

The spin doctors talked about converting waste into nutrient-rich fertiliser, to be implemented on a drive-in, drive-out basis. The dump trucks would enter the facility along a tree-lined avenue that angled down to a basement area, where they unload and exit out the other side of the building via another tree-lined thoroughfare. The ground floor would be leased out to new-age businesses with a green focus—plus a theme park, of course.

"This is all we need, a theme park," lamented Andrew, with his feet in a basin of hot water. No one expected the flu season to arrive early, and he also had a frog in his throat. That's about as green as Andy would ever be.

"I don't know, darling. It might be Dog World. Mac would love that."

The success of the project surprised everyone. The facility produced so much fertiliser; the landscaping people spread it all around the perimeter of the council property, for many years an eyesore. In a few months, the place resembled a jungle paradise and became a target destination for romantic liaisons, dog walkers, and botanical purists. The new version of Lavender Avenue boasted lush nature strips and attractive flowers dotted along the footpath. Kathy and Andrew now owned the worst house on the best street. The value of their home soared.

So did the rental prices on the ground floor of the development, which was tough luck for the green focus. Retailers now represented included designer outlets and high-end stores. Chic restaurants and multi-cultural food malls appeared, all offering free underground parking. Every motorist was entitled to depart with a bag of fertiliser in his trunk; also gratis. The contract for the last available commercial space in the complex was inked only days before I started this story—a franchise known as Krispy Kreme Doughnuts. Over to you, Mac.

THE BENT OBJECT

I awoke in a bit of a state the morning after the night before. Cognac is a picturesque town in Southwest France, but it is not a place to recover from a hangover. Everywhere you look, there is evidence of alcohol. The inn where I stayed was owned by Brandy Alexander, and this is the location where St. Bernard rescue dogs come for their training.

This stopover was not a planned destination. My car had broken down the previous afternoon, and the road service took some time to reach me. I advised them that my misfortune had occurred just outside the town of Ralentir, only to later discover that this is a French word meaning "slow down." The locals suggested a comfortable *bistrot* to pass the hours, and this sojourn led to my inebriated state.

Brandy owned a dog, a small spaniel called Rémy. The bitch possessed quite a bit of character, but she didn't like me (I'm talking about the pooch). This indifference might have been because, in my drunken stupor, I may have stepped on her while trying to locate my room. At least her owner talked to me, and we chewed the fat as we savoured the area's favourite tipple. I didn't realise the woman had a drinking problem. Out of earshot, they referred to her as Alexander the Grape.

The inn more or less ran itself, which gave the lady time to visit her friend in a nearby town. Regularly, Brandy and Rémy would join Princess Priscilla for lunch at the brasserie on the banks of the Charente River. Cilla always brought along her cat, Martin.

The gal wasn't really a princess, but people in her village regarded her as royalty, so she lived with the appellation. Would you believe that on the second day after I arrived, the two ladies managed to get themselves on the TV news? While enjoying their meal, they spied a headless body floating down the stream.

I know what you're thinking, but the government outlawed the use of the guillotine in 1981. This scenario provided a writer with all the ingredients for a murder mystery, so I decided to stick around and see what eventuated. To provide support, I accompanied my landlady to the police station, where, in the absence of Bloodhounds, they accepted Mrs Alexander's offer of a canine's opinion regarding the identification of the corpse. Rémy sniffed about for a minute or two and then retreated to the corner of the room. The gendarme in charge believed he already knew the name of the victim.

"Le corps, Madame, est Président Serge Benattar."

"Sacre Bleu," gasped Brandy. "The head of state!"

Yes, even without a head, the president of France proved to be recognisable. All of Paris knew about the tattoo of Joan of Arc on his bottom, but what was he doing in the Charente district?

Can I let the cat out of the bag? The police understood exactly what he did on their patch. The fellow owned a house in the region, which he used for entertaining his mistress. The bodyguard detail was aware of this, as were the local gendarmes. Even Priscilla knew about it, but being a discreet person, kept that knowledge to herself, unlike those who loved to gossip. Mistress Holly, a Canadian, could not be found.

As you might expect, with the identity of the victim revealed to the media, all available newshounds headed for Cognac. The rush was on to find the president's head and his mistress. All of Brandy's rooms were booked, and Rémy revelled in the attention she received. If the victim's noggin smelled the same as his torso, the dog might be the first to track it down. For the moment, the lady charged twenty euros for a photo opportunity with either of them.

When you consider the exploits of Dupin, Lupin, Maigret, and Inspector Clouseau, you would think the French Sûreté might crack the case, but even the greatest detectives have trouble with headless bodies. One of the most outrageous views involved the Loch Ness Monster visiting from Scotland. Others pointed the finger at South American headhunters. However, the popular belief put his wife in the frame big time.

Was the woman aware of the relationship between her husband and the junior diplomat from the Canadian Embassy? Probably, but that doesn't make her a killer. Nevertheless, you might consider the first lady's former profession in the wine trade, where she became an exponent of Sabrage, opening Champagne bottles with a sword.

The coroner revealed that the cut was clean and may have been generated by an enraged crazy person of either sex. Other injuries were blamed on the fish in the river, although several fishermen maintained there were no fish in the river. Certainly, market prices would indicate that.

The station sergeant received a verbal commendation for identifying the body, but his part in the investigation was downgraded. With the homicide boys in town, there were careers at stake. Forensics turned over the victim's residence but came up with nothing. Only then did the visitors turn to Rémy and a nose often described as wet and wonderful.

"My dog inspected the corpse, and he understands what to do," said the lady who wondered what she could charge these government lackeys for canine services. Président Benattar probably gave off the aroma of stale liquor more than anything else. The guy liked to party when given his head.

From my recollections, the last person to have his head on a platter was John the Baptist, and he had no connection with Élysée politicking whatsoever. His involvement with a dance hall debutante called Salome led to his downfall. In French politics, you dance with the devil, or you don't succeed, and that is why the *chef de l'État* tried to avoid his many enemies. The wife may have been first in the queue but there were others with malicious intent, including the Prime Minister.

"The stupid cow lost his head over a femme fatale. Now he has lost his head, period. What an idiot!"

All this vitriol was part of an outburst that included a high degree of profanity. I have done my best to interpret it in a manner that will not offend. All the same, the fellow should be rated on the list of possible assassins, even though he resided a long way from the scene of the crime. Finding answers closer to home might be the way to go, so I questioned the owner of the animal we have all come to love.

"Tell me, Brandy, has Rémy come up with a perp yet? She has been poking her nose all around town and getting fat on the freebies."

The dog had indeed been busy, but the president's odour was nowhere. The head of the investigation, Michel LeBlanc, was also frustrated. Perhaps it is time to analyse this doyen of detectives. In the same manner as Maigret, he sucked on his pipe and counted the follicles as they fell from his head. The man, a legend in his lifetime, might see time as his enemy. Would this be his last case? Who can forget the way he solved the mystery of "The blue cheese that turned green?" Or his ongoing encounters with Pierre the Bear, the cat burglar from Montmartre.

At this time, there was interest in a thief called the "Tooth Fairy," who was gay but not happy. The fellow had been a mild-mannered dentist in the suburbs until he botched a root canal procedure and found himself in court. He went rogue and started stealing gold fillings from people, whether they were dead or alive. Because Président Benattar exhibited so much glitter in his mouth, it would have been easier and quicker to lop off his head and remove the goodies at a later date.

The spin doctors at the Élysée Palace were having none of that. They wanted to declare war on Australia. You may not have heard about this, but a few years ago, the Aussies welched on a submarine deal, and relations had been poor ever since. However, Serge Benattar prepared to extend the olive branch in exchange for new trade opportunities, and a visit to the land Down Under had been slotted for late June. You would never guess how the ruler of seventy million people planned to surprise his hosts.

He was learning to throw the boomerang.

His teacher, Trevor Frith, was a security guard attached to the Australian consulate. When I say security guard, I mean the hush-hush kind. The fellow was an intelligence officer with a heart of gold, as most Australians have. Every morning before breakfast, he would meet *le Président de la République* in the gardens, and they would practise with the wooden whistler. The main man proved to be quite adept at it.

So much for my rumour and hearsay overload. The big news was that the mistress had turned up, having walked into her embassy as she always did at 9 a.m. on a Monday. Michel LeBlanc was called back from Cognac to conduct the interview.

"Bonjour, mademoiselle. Je suis Inspecteur LeBlanc de la Sûreté."

"And hello to you, inspector. Why don't we speak English? You are capable, yes?"

"Of course," said the taken-aback lawman. This woman seemed assured and confident, and he wondered how much she knew. Questions would have to be direct and to the point.

"Can you confirm that you spent the recent weekend with the president?"

"What president would that be, sir?"

Oh dear, thought the investigator. Everyone in Paris knew she was having it off with SB except herself. How long would this subterfuge last for?

"Please don't waste my time. Serge Benattar is dead, and you are a prime suspect. Tell me when you last saw the victim."

Holly deliberated, as you do when you are trying to think on your feet. She expected this inquisitor would be more than competent at his job, but she had nothing to hide. Or did she?

"Alright, inspector. I did spend Friday and Saturday with SB, but I departed on Sunday morning to visit the Angeleum market on my way back to Paris. When I left him, he was heading for the riverbank to practise his boomerang throwing."

"Boomerang! What is this boomerang?"

"It is an Australian weapon used by Indigenous people. If you throw the thing correctly, it comes back to you. Serge was good at it and often hurled the wooden stick under the Chateauneuf Bridge, so it would return over the bridge. All these skills he learned from an Aussie in their embassy."

And so Michel LeBlanc met Trevor Frith.

"This wooden instrument you show me. It has razor-sharp edges."

"That is correct," said Trevor, in an explanatory mood. "We have hunting boomerangs, tourist boomerangs, and military models. I'm afraid I can't tell you about the latter—national security. My palace student practised with a military model, which is all we have in stock over here. I told him that as long as he used gloves, he wouldn't hurt himself."

For three hours after he left the Aussie embassy, LeBlanc sat in his office, staring at the wall, dumbfounded. Finally, he reached for the phone and dialled the precinct in Cognac.

"Sergeant, I want you to get that woman and her dog and scour the waterway near the president's residence. Give me a "Head's Up" if you find anything. Don't go to the media."

The inspector was proud of his English and liked to experiment with all the idioms. In this case, the idiom used might be regarded as tasteless.

It took some time, but the sniffing beast found what they were looking for. The head had been decapitated by the boomerang and fallen in the shallows to become lodged in some crags underwater. Searchers discovered the bent object nearby.

The canine from Cognac!

In the ensuing months, Rémy, Martin, Brandy, and Priscilla continued their relationship at the brasserie by the river. I am still in custody for writing such a silly story.

ABOUT THE AUTHOR

Gerry Burke received a Jesuit-inspired education at Xavier College in Melbourne, Australia, where he still lives. Before commencing his long career in advertising, the author was employed by an international mining company, which included a three-year stint in New Guinea. He also dabbled in the horse-racing industry, as an owner and breeder, with some success. Being a former accountant and advertising creative, no one expected Gerry to become a published author, but he embraced this initiative to stave off dementia.

He has since penned six novels, seven volumes of short stories, and two offerings of commentary and opinion relating to politics, entertainment, sport and travel. The PEST pseudonym was subjected to a sea change with the introduction of popular discount detective Paddy Pest to booklovers everywhere.

Most people see the garrulous gumshoe from Down Under as a cross between James Bond and Maxwell Smart, and he has been the protagonist in a number of the author's humour-laden publications. In recent times, there have been diversions into Science Fiction and absolute fiction, all of which have won enthusiastic acclaim.

Mr. Burke's credentials have been well established, with eleven of his books featuring as a winner or finalist in a variety of international literary competitions. Three volumes have received multiple citations.

Gerry is single and lives with photographs of his best racehorses.
http://gerryburke.net

This book would not have been possible without the co-operation of my friends and their dogs. I thank those below for their contribution.

Atticus	Kevin Cronin
Baloo	Ken Craigie
Billy	Sally O'Gorman
Dusty/Honey	Trevor Frith
Chubbs	Dominque Gauci
Finnegan	Melinda Brewer
LeBron	Amanda Soogun
Louie	Gail Dee
Maciato	Andrew Mularczyk/Kathy Johnston
Thelma Lou/Ralphie	Joan Crumpler
Pepe/Coco Pop	Denver Jansz
Rémy	Holly/Steve Kent
Rocky	Ron Stokes
Sophie	Helen Moreland

Baloo & Rehnu

Atticus & Kevin

Billy & Sally

Louie & Gail / Coco Pop & Denver

Mac & Kathy

Sophie & Helen

Finnegan & Melinda

Rémy & Holly

AUTHOR'S PREVIOUS WORKS

AMERICAN FICTION AWARDS–FINALIST
Sky Foil - an international conspiracy
The Europeans - a saga of settlement Down Under
My Book of Revelations - stories that burst the bubble of believability

BOOK EXCELLENCE AWARDS–FINALIST
Citizen Vain - stories from Down Under and all over
My Book of Revelations - stories that burst the bubble of believability
The Europeans - a saga of settlement Down Under
The Snoodle Contract - a provocative power play of political perfidy
The Replicants - they come in peace or so they say
Be Dead and Be Damned - murder with malice in Melbourne

BEST BOOK AWARDS–FINALIST
Citizen Vain - stories from Down Under and all over
My Book of Revelations - stories that burst the bubble of believability
Pest Takes a Chance - and other humorous stories
Pest on the Run - more humorous short stories
The Hero of Hucklebuck Drive - another Paddy Pest mystery

DA VINCI EYE AWARD–FINALIST
Citizen Vain - stories from Down Under and all over

INDEPENDENT PUBLISHER BRONZE MEDAL
Paddy's People - tales of life, love, laughter, and smelly horses

PINNACLE ACHIEVEMENT AWARD–BEST BOOK/ SHORT STORIES
Citizen Vain - stories from Down Under and all over

SHORT STORIES, COMMUTERS' COMPANION & OPINION PIECES
Down Under Shorts - stories to read while they're fumigating your pants
The Lady on the Train - more humorous Paddy Pest yarns
From Beer to Paternity - one man's journey through life as we know it

Printed in the United States
by Baker & Taylor Publisher Services

Printed in the United States
by Baker & Taylor Publisher Services